Wild Wind

Poems and Stories Inspired by
the Songs of Robert Earl Keen

LEXINGTON, KENTUCKY - AUGUST 29: Robert Earl Keen performs during the 2021 Railbird Festival at Keeneland Racecourse on August 29, 2021 in Lexington, Kentucky. (Photo by Stephen J. Cohen/Getty Images)

Wild Wind

Poems and Stories Inspired by
the Songs of Robert Earl Keen

edited by
Sandra Johnson Cooper
and Ron Cooper

Lake Dallas, Texas

Copyright © 2024 by Sandra Johnson Cooper and Ron Cooper
All rights reserved
Printed in the United States of America

FIRST EDITION

Requests for permission to reprint material from this collection should be directed to:

Permissions
Madville Publishing
P.O. Box 358
Lake Dallas, TX 75065

Cover Design and Typesetting: Kimberly Davis
Cover Art: Licensed through Shutterstock
Copyedit: Stetson Cooper

ISBN: 978-1-963695-01-4 paperback,
978-1-963695-02-1 ebook
Library of Congress Control Number: 2024946800

Contents

Preface — vii
Introduction — ix

Alan Birkelbach — 1
   "Barbeque—Lucifer Contemplates Barbeque"

Rick Campbell — 3
   "No Kinda Dancer"
   "The Road Goes On Forever"
   "Feeling Good Again"

Greg Clary — 6
   "Dreadful Selfish Crime—(One Last Time)"

Andrew E. Coats — 7
   "Corpus Christi Bay—Southern god of Sobriety"

Sandra Johnson Cooper — 9
   "Willie—Fox Rain"

Rupert Fike — 11
   "Furnace Fan"—A Lizard's Response

Cal Freeman — 13
   "Feeling Good Again"

Carol Parris Krauss — 15
   "The Front Porch Song—Any Porch, Any Place"

karla k. morton — 16
   "That Buckin' Song—That Buckskin You Loved"

Jeff Newberry — 17
   "Gringo Honeymoon—The Cowboy's Tale"

Garrison M. Somers "I Gotta Go" "Not a Drop of Rain"	19
Heath Bowen "Gone On"	23
Michael Amos Cody "Carolina"	35
Ron Cooper "Wild Wind"	47
Sandra Johnson Cooper "The Road Goes on Forever"	60
Donna Wojnar Dzurilla "Christabel"	63
Patrick Michael Finn "Broken End of Love"	69
Scott Gould The Five Pound Bass—Every Sunday	72
Bobby Horecka "Corpus Christi Bay—Just One of the Band"	78
Patti Meredith "No Kinda Dancer—Phantom Partner"	88
Kimberly Parish Davis "Willie"	96
Janna Jones "Feelin' Good Again—Waiting for You"	105
Contributors	125

Preface

When we moved from Bend, Oregon to Austin, Texas, in the fall of '96, we made a stop in Idaho on the way. My dad received a newsletter from Robert Earl Keen saying he had a new live album out, so we decided to stop in Boise at a music store on the off chance they might have a copy on cassette. This was when tapes were being replaced by CDs and they were becoming hard to find. There was only one tape in the country "K" section—it was *No. 2 Live Dinner*. We put that tape in the cassette player and we didn't stop listening to it until we got to Austin. I'm not exaggerating. Once in a while we would pop something else in and make it a few songs into the album, and then switch back to *No. 2 Live Dinner*. It was that good. And twenty years later, it's still that good. It's my favorite live album of all time.

When we got to Austin, we looked Robert up, since dad had known him from a distance for twenty years or so. (Dad was the first artist to ever cut one of REK's songs, "Willie Boy"). He almost immediately took us under his wing and took us on the road with him, talking highly of the band, and in many ways mentored us while making us feel like we were more seasoned and significant than we actually were, especially at the time. He offered me songwriting advice and influenced me to pour over and vary the set list every night—something not many artists do.

Robert and his wife, Kathleen, even managed us for a couple years. To say Robert Earl helped us out in the early years would be a massive understatement.

Robert and all the guys in the band have always gone above and beyond to make our band and family feel welcome and at home, especially on stage. We've been lucky enough to open more than a hundred shows over the last twenty-seven years, and I'm pretty sure I watched every single one of them. Their influence on us and our generation of Texas musicians is incalculable.

They've supported us from the second we set our suitcases down till the last chord of their final song, and we couldn't be more honored to have shared so many moments along the way and to be lucky enough to call them friends.

Standing backstage at his final show at John T. Flores Country Store in Helotes just before he led a big group encore singalong, Robert asked me if I knew the words to "Not Fade Away." I said, "Yep. What verse do you want me to do?" to which he replied, "All of em—those are the ones I don't know." REK is one funny SOB. It was a surreal, full circle moment I'll never forget.

We'll always be indebted to Robert for all he's done for Reckless Kelly and our generation of Texas musicians, and although he retired from live performances about a year ago, I have a feeling he'll be back at it someday… He's just too damn good not to.

Willy Braun, Reckless Kelly

Introduction

About 1989, Ron first heard a Robert Earl Keen song on WMNF Community Radio in Tampa, Florida. This station plays much alternative music, and Ron even did a few shows at the station, substituting for DJs who had to cancel their shows. The song was Keen's cover of Blackie Farrell's "Sonora's Death Row," not even one that Keen himself had penned. Ron, however, loved the song so much that he was excited to see Keen in concert in Tampa along with songwriting legends Townes Van Zandt and Guy Clark. Keen was just beginning to get a following, and while he was obviously in awe of the elder craftsmen, he deeply impressed Ron by holding his own when he joined Van Zandt and Clark on stage and swapped songs and jokes.

Soon after, Sandra first heard "The Road Goes on Forever," and she was instantly as much a fan as Ron. She sent her brother Tom an REK CD, and Tom was hooked as well. Months later he drove down from South Carolina for a concert in Florida, and we waited for several hours at a local record store where REK was scheduled to appear to sign items before the concert. Unfortunately, REK was delayed and could not make the signing. Later we struck up a conversation with the owner of the venue, who told us to wait at the bar. We'd planned to do that anyway and were confused about what the owner was up to, but soon REK emerged through a side door and hollered, "Tom? Tom Johnson?" Keen apologized that Tom had driven so far and missed him earlier, and he offered an autographed shirt and a hug. Over three decades later, Tom still cherishes that shirt and the memory of REK's warmth and generosity of spirit. Since then, Ron and Sandra have attended at least fifteen Robert Earl Keen concerts and are each time delighted with how he brings something new to every performance.

The idea for this anthology began years ago as a collection of essays from various academic perspectives—philosophical, literary, psychological, sociological, etc. A number of scholars were on board, ready to offer their analyses of how this songwriter creates and transfers so much cultural currency. However, the project stalled, largely because of the concern that the essays would be too highfalutin' and stodgy (as academic writing tends to be!) and of interest only to other academics, not something that REK's fans would find appealing. Switching instead to literature inspired by REK's work has proved to be a much more exciting project. The talented writers who contributed to this collection include long-time followers of REK's work as well as some who are recent fans. Some extended a song's narrative in unexpected trajectories, some retold the story from the perspective of a minor character (in one case a lizard!), and some gave the lyrics ingenious (even other-worldly) interpretations.

Each piece here takes its title from the REK song that inspired it. Where an author supplied his or her own title, it was added to the song title. We hope that readers will not only enjoy the contents but also seek out other work by these terrific writers with whom we are honored to collaborate.

Sandra Johnson Cooper and Ron Cooper

Poetry

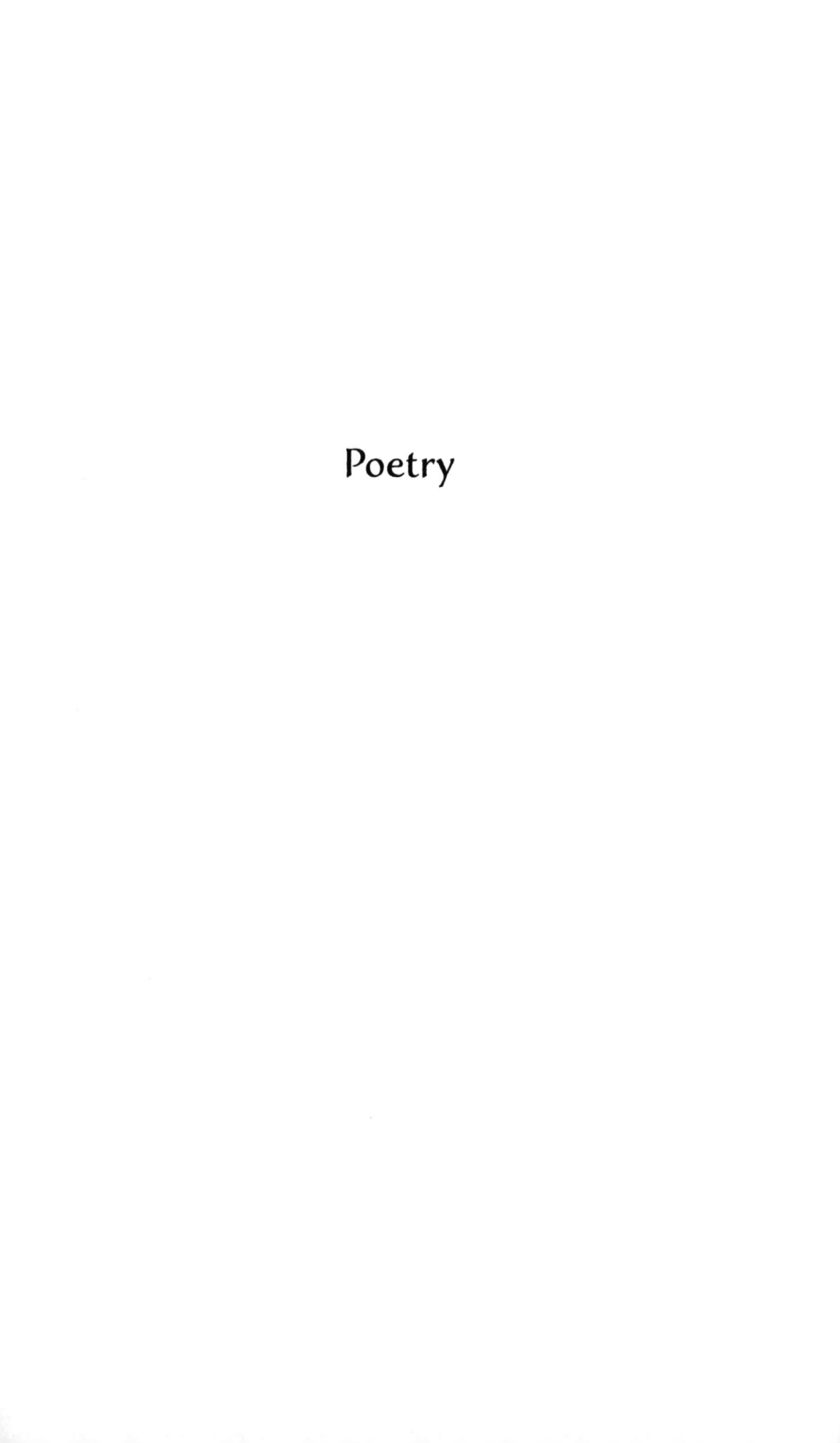

Alan Birkelbach

"Barbeque—Lucifer Contemplates Barbeque"

*(With thanks, apologies, and acknowledged inspiration
to Robert Earl Keen and John Milton)*

Say what you will. Of course, he knows of this
dark, smoky stronghold. His reason and his vision
are limitless. He sees and counts each deepest,
furrowed brow, each tired, sullied wing.
And that is all the honor I can pay.
It has been writ my falling, flaming arc
was epic, legendary (yes, I boast),
perhaps even scouring and fatal, but
after all, I am immortal with
all senses, mind, and malice eternally intact.

So, as I contemplated the myriad forms
of scowling, armed revenge, I was aware
of the very charred wood underfoot,
the oak and mesquite, and all creatures around
me, hair seared, mouths agape, dull and so
potentially delicious. Perhaps, I thought,
perhaps there is more than one way to tempt.
After all, most evil is a nebulous,
transitory thing. It's flesh darling.
I could make use of it. So, out of all
the sins here's where we are: lust and gluttony.
Two of my favorites. And a drink
called Big Red. How delightful.

As it turns out this was indeed the clime,
the region and the soil. It's true. I do

have a charcoal pit and an exceptional fire.
It is a legacy thing. I take some pride in it.

If there were angels who decried against
the meat then I should have had to chastise them
for am I not the prince who did rebel,
son of the morning star, the red-eyed
eternal pit boss? Humans! Listen!
It is all you need to hear: this fare
will make you young again. But inside I
will think, as I have thought through many racks
and flames: what robust rebirth is this viand
for all shallow-limbed mortals,
crucibled in fire, making all
unsettled hearts set aside aspirations
of ascension? They will acknowledge their
level of divinity—or lack of.
Yes, it is that necessary and good.

I do not need an angelic sword to carve
these dripping slices. Tis better to serve barbeque
in Hell than to scoop tepid cheese
fondue in Heaven. I tell you this: Taste.
Swallow. Be someone. Set yourself on fire.

Rick Campbell

"No Kinda Dancer"

My friend said she married her husband
because she liked the way he danced. I said I
can dance. I can do the twist, the stomp, the
mashed potato too. Any old dance that you
want to do. She said you're no kinda dancer.

Maybe I'm no kinda dancer, but come on,
let's dance, put on your red shoes and dance.
There's never been a dance that's so easy to
do. It even makes you happy when you're
 feelin blue. Summer's here and the time
is right for dancing in the street.

Yea, I'm no kinda dancer, but do you wanna dance and hold my
hand? We could be dancing, dancing in the dark, could be literally waltzing on air if you save the last dance for me.

"The Road Goes On Forever"

As Sherry often did, as perhaps many would, she
looked back on that day when her life changed forever,
for the good perhaps, who's to say? She shot the cop in
the alley and Sonny gave her a bag of money and then
drove away. She went back home, which some might
find surprising, and bought a new Mercedes, which some might
find obvious and reckless. She's riding
down Main Street, down to the river, with a cold beer
between her legs. Some might wonder why she did not
have a cooler or put the beer on the floor. Was it to remember or to
forget? She's seen the paper. Sonny's
going to the chair. Florida, Raiford probably. Maybe
she's thinking of how Sonny changed her life when he
laid that tourist out with his cue stick and they blew
that popsicle town and headed to Miami where he
knew some guys who knew some guys who could get
them what they needed to make sure the party never ends.

"Feeling Good Again"

I don't need no blues.
No silly submarine songs.
Just left my dog dead down
on the vet's beige tile floor. Driving
south through pine woods, sand forest
roads cutting right and left, river
somewhere west of palmetto hammocks.
Then I get it. He reaches into his pocket,
finds three twenties and a ten.
His girl comes, wanted but unexpected,
down the bar room stairs. I'm feeling good,
like maybe this is a new good.
Like the days go on, white birds
in a blue, blue sky. Forty miles
down Smith Creek Road,
Rose Street, Sopchoppy Highway,
then Surf Road take me home.

Greg Clary

"Dreadful Selfish Crime—(One Last Time)"

Seems like yesterday
that coming and going
didn't matter much.
Until I no longer could.
She stopped by, unannounced,
for a short trip
to a far-away place.
We ignored the mirror
reflecting our missed chances
and all the flinches
that had rebuilt our faces.
Our pasts nothing
but stray cats
roaming unleashed
through the alleys
of our memories,
reminders of our
impermanent passion,
lingering sorrow,
and unfinished regret.

Andrew E. Coats

"Corpus Christi Bay—Southern god of Sobriety"

Morning glories, inglorious morning
Moonflowers die in the midday sun
There I lay, fetal condition
Wheeze of apnea, Ambien hung

No hose of hypoxia, Nova's Hydroxia
Just trying to box out the day
Brother and I, face down on the porch again
Along the docks of Corpus Christi Bay

The old bluesman, John Dee, once told me, "You've got to hold on to the grass to keep from fallin' off the ground."

And goddamit tomorrow's Monday, which means:

Avalanche of commitment
Tornado of decision
Hurricane of confliction
Earthquake of completion

<u>Will</u>: where has my will gone hunting?
<u>Drive</u>: drive me to the moon, you say?
<u>Discipline</u>: discipline me with the large paddle.
<u>Energy</u>: teach me how $E = mc^2$.

Each day, the circle closes.
Each day, the cycle repeats.
Each day, eternal recurrence.
Each day, hard to the feat.

"The only easy day was yesterday",
Isn't that what the SEALs say?

Every day, I lean to the left of the bed.
And try to pray . . . but to what?
Whatever gods might stumble this way?
To this: the Southern god of sobriety.

Here in Corpus Christi Bay.

Sandra Johnson Cooper

"Willie—Fox Rain"

Had I known then—a girl in Incheon, watching the shirtless American soldier
loading crates into the parade of jeeps, headed South—
of the dryness of the West Texas dirt, I might have turned back to my father's paulownia table.
Born by the sea, I knew the danger of standing too long in the sun, yet I stood on the sand and watched his broad back redden,
felt my mouth parch from the heat of that day, of that sun. I giggled at his
low, throaty growl.

Invited to tea with my father, he crouched on all fours to fit. His brow knitted at the pomegranate-tinged leaves. My father talked of sun-showers, and the marriage of the fox and the tiger. The soldier left after red tea and proposals.
I look through the screen door, see the clouds moving in even as the sun beats down on the bone-dry dirt, and know he'll be home. Soon.
What did I know in Incheon of clouds, of silver chains, of a man crouching by the side of the bed, snapping at my wrist?

I rise from his mesquite table, go to the sink to fill the pot with water and add the tea, feel the limp, fruitless bags
and remember an American story about the Devil beating his wife
during a sunny, rainy day.

He'll need a cold glass after he untacks and curries Willie.
What did I know then, chasing the shirtless American soldier,
running between the tides, of the deserts that exist between a
  people,
between a man and woman?
What did I know of a place where rains are as dry as sand?

Rupert Fike

"Furnace Fan"—A Lizard's Response
—I understand why lizards live in sunny Arizona,
why people do and call it home, I'll never understand.

It's hurtful enough we're always referred to as "cold-blooded"
   (the mindset of murderers), but now this condescension
from someone we never thought would treat us this-a-way—
   saying you "understand" lizard folk when the innate craft
of our daily lives is beyond two-legged comprehension,
   that constant series of adjustments we have to make
(sun to shade; shade to sun) to maintain proper body temps,
   the everyday dance your kind can't possibly "understand,"
humans with your famous four chamber heart, the heat pump
   that allows you to get by with puffy coats in winter
while we're slink-skinking around in search of some rejuvenating
   sun where we can reflect on our body-positive traits
like the chameleonic ability to blend in wherever
   or our Lazarus-like regeneration of new tails.
Not to mention the length, speed and dexterity
   of our tongues (a prowess your kind surely covets).
Yet you are correct that sunny Arizona's no joke, especially
   when you got to your Scottsdale gig "way too early"
and "sat around for hours" playing smush-ball out on
   the 110-degree egg-frying, bacon-frying parking lot
while eating Uncle Joe's scorching hot chicken wings—so yes,
   it *was* hot, but you brought some of that shit on yourself!
The smush-ball game growing so, ahem, heated a roadie left
   the trailer door open--shade spotted!—my chance to crawl
up into a speaker box and cool down, the load-in suddenly
   starting, me getting jostle-toted into The River Room,
the AC so freezing I slipped into slow-mode before the amps
   warmed me up enough to notice your usual rowdies
whooping and crowding in, their ciggy smoke so thick

I had to use my double-hinged eyelids (animal kingdom's best!)
to cut through the haze and see where I was—on stage
    where it was showtime, me singing along with everybody
else to that Norman Blake tune you love to open with,
    his sins, same as all our sins, of the overtaking variety,
the whole room laughing at that long story of your old rancher
    landlord showing up to holler, "Robert Keen, Robert Keen!"
before making you go buck bales or fence or round up strays,
    and the love was flowing, empty Amber Bock bottles rolling,
clink-clanking down the aisles, everything reminding me how much
    I get you, how much I need to just let go of perceived slights
now that we're touring together, me stowing away in my speaker,
    hitching a ride to the next show where two monitor cousins
are waiting in the Bakersfield parking lot hoping I'll comp them,
    toggling on the asphalt from sun to shade; shade to sun,
the two-step we never quit stepping, species coming,
    species going, an ice-age here, a meteor die-off there,
and us the constant, out-living dinosaurs and soon to out-last
    you-people, our party the one that truly goes on forever.

Cal Freeman

"Feeling Good Again"

Easter Sunday, east side of Detroit, backyard of Carol's bungalow.
John Shelley was playing Robert Earl Keen songs on the garage stereo.
I'd had a near nervous breakdown at the all night Chinese café
downtown Good Friday night while considering my alcohol intake.
Now we were shooting blended Canadian whiskey and drinking
    High Lifes.
Al's workbench was set up as a provisional bar; we'd pound our shot
    glasses
on the swivel vise before we took a shot. Whenever one of us
got thirsty, we'd knock on the side window of that once-car garage
and sing, "Knock on the window, cheers on the vise, nah nah nah
    nah,"
until someone produced the bottle and filled another round.
Shelley played "The Road Goes on Forever" a time or two,
but "Feeling Good Again" was the song for that day, for that moment,
for the nascent spring. Carol and Jennie got drunk and Al got drunk
and Pat the bartender who hadn't drank in decades played with Al's
pit bull Caesar on the back porch and sang along with the hook
while laughing at everyone getting drunk at Carol Shanku's Easter
    party.
Across the river, in Windsor, Ontario, Hiram Walker was listening
to Robert Earl Keen and singing along with us. That voice
with its little rasp unadorned on those small Bose speakers,
and I don't remember dinner. We all felt the ham and kielbasa and
    kraut
could wait since the weather was so good. While the ostensive love
of music is love, and the ostensive love of God is often not,
a few songs put over right can make you believe in something again.
The city golf course across the two-lane road had just woken
into swamp thistle and purple loosestrife. They were teeing up

platitudes about spring and resurrection. We were singing and
    drinking,
we who with every shot got worse, we who couldn't listen to
    ourselves
listening to the songs we sang along to on a holiday that gives
no buffer between the work of suffering and celebration.

Carol Parris Krauss

"The Front Porch Song—Any Porch, Any Place"

I come from a long, but crooked line of mountaineers
mixed with a few alcoholics. A passel of porch people.
Sitting on a two-step stoop with crumbling corners. Rebar
poking my ass while sipping a cheap chablis out of one of
    Granny's wine glasses.
Cross-legged on the garage floor shucking corn, cursing silks.
Snapping green beans as darkness scoots over the Piedmont.
Teetering on the tailgate of a F-150 outside Death Valley,
    Clemson SC.
Nibbling soggy pimento cheese sandwiches. Cursing the
    Tommy Bowden years.
That time at the kitchen table when the rain threatened to push
    the house
to the Elizabeth River. Set her to sailing after already taking
    away the power.
Reading a sappy novel by the only light to be found.
At school, grading essays with the Virginia sun over my shoulder.
An aching back, numb butt, and ink smudged hands.
My people conjure our porches. Occasionally we happen upon
    a wide planked
beauty with rocking chairs a plenty, but most any place where
    we gather
wool, work through the work, and push toward play is a porch.

karla k. morton

"That Buckin' Song—That Buckskin You Loved"

Maybe heaven is a meant-to-be-place
where dogs live forever,
and horses have wings—
black points on the tips,
and F-16's bombed the Romans
before they could crucify Jesus.

Maybe you're there now
a fresh cocktail in hand,
your best friend asking
What the hell took you so long.

Jeff Newberry

"Gringo Honeymoon—The Cowboy's Tale"

He blew a smoke ring and he smiled at us. "I ain't never goin' back."
—"Gringo Honeymoon"

In my mind, it was all tan dust and sepia towns
with saloons where swinging doors admit
six-gun-armed cowboys who sip whiskey
from brass cups dreaming of high noon shootouts.

This one-room shack with a sour cot and empty
bottles rolling across the hardwood floor
recall less that life and more the tedium
I once thought I'd escaped: home, family,

the bore of daily chores, taking out garbage
you make more of the next day. I got away,
fled south. Sold grass to gringos to pass
the time between weekend drunks and hookers.

The wrong man buys a dime bag. I'm lost
down here now, where Pancho got left
south of the border. That old song and dance—
no way back into the life that folded

behind me like a barroom door at last call.
I pawned a wedding band and bought a gunbelt
that fits too tight. A couple finds me on afternoon,
asks about the Rio Grande. Says *honeymoon*.

Says *adventure*. Says it all with clasped hands
and the lust of youth clouding their eyes.
I'm never going back. I can never go back.
When they disappear in a haze of smoke

and light beer, headed father south still,
I think of how songs once written imply and end.
Every chorus stops. The chords run out.
You play it again, hoping it'll change. It won't.

Garrison M. Somers

"I Gotta Go"

Grim Herodotus never bothered
to explicate to we mere mortals
what to do when our heroes
leave, without saying a word.
With uncomfortable speed
summer poppies bloom and fade.
A gardener intentionally spills
patiently gathered seed.
Hopeful eyes tilt skyward,
praying for some vague sign,
wasting not, wanting… everything,
blinking, squinting, tear-blurred.
It matters nothing that He casts
on fields of stone or thorn,
because all is short, from
a certain place, nothing lasts.
So scribe your next rhyme
and stride onto the stage,
loudly sing their old songs,
then bow, one more time.
And late, near day's being done,
put feet up, sip your drink, breathe.
What difference, really, whether
son buries father, or father buries son.

"Not a Drop of Rain"

Don't use the word poetry around the man.
He will not deny it, but may turn his back
on you for spouting something so highbrow,
so out of tune with what he is, has been, really, for so long
that this road has ruts and sprung bootheels.
Tell the man the weather report, he doesn't care
that it will all change tomorrow. Or not.
Somewhere there are calls for showers
followed by a cooling trend. It doesn't matter.
He knows what you and I only guess at.
That words aren't real, music's not real,
Only feelings are true—hunger, thirst.
He doesn't pray for what he hasn't got,
hears a different channel, flips bicycles
into a hat, snaps blue tips alight and blows them out
just to smell the sulfur smoke,
remembers the eyes of a certain girl,
wonders if she still loves slow dancing, smiles
as he sits on front porch steps and squints at the sky
which has never let him down, always hot, always dry.

Fiction

Heath Bowen

"Gone On"

Bobby Joe fought like hell to keep Mary from being anything other than a good lay. Naked, voluptuous, and salacious, she often left him to ache all over. She was more trouble than she was worth. Mary was a good lay. For Bobby, it was best to keep it as simple as that.

When they weren't fooling around, they were drinking, and Bobby and Mary loved to drink. In between beer and bourbon, Mary pushed men. She loved knowing she could drive a man to become Undone. She loved the honeymoon making-up. She owned them as surely as if her name was tattooed on their arms.

Bobby's mama had taught him to never hit a woman. He'd knocked out plenty of men in his day, but once Bobby learned something, unlearning it wasn't a thing. Mary might be able to tempt many a man with her slithery tongue and jukebox hips, but getting Bobby to go against his training wasn't one of them.

Mary was a wild one. Always cussing through her charcoal-colored lips like she was spitting fire. Her frayed, brown curls framed her face as her curves threatened to bust the seams of her t-shirt she had cut into a deep V. Those she passed couldn't help but do a double take, as her breasts weren't nothing short of a walking advertisement for country music.

The first time Bobby Joe had seen her, he took a long look. He took to her like she was pot liquor, she was addictive with moonshine in her eyes, weed in her hips, and lips like speed. Bobby tried to remember she was a pleasant distraction, a girl to drown out the chaos with the creaking noise of the night. He found himself addicted, couldn't get enough of the way she moved.

Bobby Joe'd always been trapped in the throes of turmoil. He'd never let himself far enough away from all the noise to make sense of it all, let alone escape it. Living in a backwoods town, miles off I-65, hadn't exactly been conducive to upward mobility. Pine Hollow was nothing but a collection of dollar stores hidden between endless rows of corn visible from the interstate. It had a school that resembled more a gathering of one-room trailers surrounding a lunchroom and bathrooms than the traditional image of a cozy red-brick schoolhouse. Crumbling warehouses neighbored a honky-tonk named Glenda's Pool Hall tavern, while atop the hill sat a church overlooking rows of scattered trailer homes and old '60s ranch-style starter houses.

And Hollow's Ridge. Hollow's Ridge was a steep cliff past the trailer that overlooked an abandoned strip mine. At the bottom of the cliff was an endless pit filled with water, rock, and the bones of those who crossed the Donny Brothers.

Bobby Joe knows the ridge. He and the other locals used to shimmy down the scrub cliff and use the scraggly baby pines to throw themselves into the pit. This was before his kin left him to fend for himself when he was sixteen. Before the Donny Brothers lured him into stripping copper wire and fighting in bare-knuckle brawls with cash and brand-new pickup trucks, and it was years before Mary walked into Glenda's in her V-neck.

Mary, with her love for the honky-tonk and her swinging hips, captured Bobby Joe's attention. The moment he saw down that V-neck, he knew he'd have to fight to keep his heart on lockdown. She loved Glenda's more than weed or alcohol, and her two-step on the dance floor could make Bobby Joe drunk. It was a backwoods reverie. Jukebox religion. Her hips swayed like she was the one who had made Hank Williams sad and lonely.

It was a sultry summer evening when their paths first crossed. She was clutching a bottle of Jack Daniels, and when Bobby Joe saw her his mouth went dry even though he was drinking PBR out of a red cup. She poured a drink from the bottle and danced with her glass through the dusty haze of the barroom floor. She shook those hips and Bobby saw what made Hank so lonesome he could cry. She looked weightless as she spun, clinging onto her bottle. Oblivious to all eyes but his, she smiled, winked, and reached out her hand.

Mary's copper-colored eyes became Bobby Joe's escape. In Mary's eyes, Bobby Joe was a catch, a good-looking big, bearded man who wore a cracked glimpse of domination. She saw beyond his rough exterior, under his calloused hands, was a good heart. It was the latter that made the former so appealing. Mary liked to feel protected by her men. She was drawn to Bobby Joe because he was genuine, but she ached for him when she found out he was dangerous.

Mary just knew she liked the looks of Bobby Joe when she beckoned him to dance. She didn't know he would be the perfect amount of mean in the dim glow of a single-wide. She might let him out the screen door at midnight, but she was still sore in the morning. She didn't know how he could leave that mark. She damn sure didn't know he had been left to raise himself after his folks abandoned him to live out West, where they replaced memories of him with cool winds and mountaintop views. They rationalized their absence as penance, they even came to speculate he had a bit of the devil in his veins.

Superstitious, like most religious people, Bobby Joe's folks decided he was possessed, and moved on after he got kicked out of school for putting a preacher's son in the hospital. They knew he was possessed because the fight started when Bobby Joe praised prostitution. He said if it weren't for a hooker there'd be no Christianity. In response, the preacher's son struck him with a King James Bible. Bobby Joe laughed and asked the preacher's son if he held up sodomy like he held up that sodomite's Bible. Bobby Joe lifted the teacher's wooden desk chair and pummeled the kid until his face was a mess of shattered bones.

Bobby Joe was sent to the Clark County Juvenile Center, and his folks took advantage of his absence by leaving. After juvie, there wasn't much work to be found for him. All the maintenance, carpentry, welding, mechanic, loading, and factory work was spread across the state, miles from Bobby Joe's home. Farm work went to family members. Jobs requiring knowledge of the trade were closed, and, anyway, any job had to be within walking distance of the trailer park. The only real chance to make any money was to work with the Donny Brothers.

The Brothers recruited him to strip copper wire and later, he grew into a bagman. Eventually, with his six-foot frame and lumberjack build, he would become their primary muscle. This position often led to violence. It also led to gym bags stuffed with enough money to buy a truck and a lot to park his trailer on.

When someone owed the Brothers, Bobby Joe would crack open a bottle with their teeth. If they still refused to pay or tried to skip town, he'd use his bat. Just seeing it on the gun rack in the back window of his F-250 was more than enough to deter people from double-crossing the Donny Brothers.

The Donny Brothers weren't actual brothers, they were cousins named Donald. After both sets of parents called it quits, the unrelated ones married each other, and the two Donalds became stepbrothers.

Both Donnies were known to be good with a weapon. Donald Jr., the older of the two, was quick with his knife, while Donald, the younger and taller, always carried a pair of brass knuckles he'd pull if he didn't like the tenor of a particular conversation.

Mary knew nothing about Bobby Joe's connection with the Donalds when they met, and she didn't really care when she found out. His violent occupation only made her want him more. She wanted her and Bobby Joe to drink bourbon and beer, and she wanted Bobby Joe to fuck her hard enough to leave a dent in the dirt underneath his single-wide.

She liked him because he was simple. He didn't force her to listen. She liked their time drinking, and the flesh on flesh that came after emptying a bottle. She knew their nights weren't going to last, but she thought she would be the one to break it off like she always did when there came talk of commitment, she didn't think it would be his job that came between them.

The night she saw Bobby Joe, the Donny Brothers had cornered him at Glenda's and pressed him into a copper-stripping job a few towns over.

"It's an abandoned housing complex," Don Jr. said. "You'll be in and out before sunrise."

"I think I'm done stripping copper," Bobby said.

"You ain't out until we say you're out," Donald said.

"But I don't feel right hauling copper no more. I got enough saved up to buy a new place outside of town."

"That don't sound like you," Don Jr. said. "Sounds like being pussy whipped to me."

"We know you been spending time with that whore," Donald said. "Don't let her make you do something stupid."

"She ain't no whore."

Don Jr. chuckled. Donald shook his head and stuck his hands into his front pockets.

"You really are a dumbfuck. Mary's been on every dick in the county."

"She ain't like that," Bobby said.

"They're all like that," Don Jr. said. "You too slow to see how fast she is."

"Don't talk about her like that," Bobby said, clenching and unclenching his fist. "You feeling froggy? You best not jump."

"Try it and see if you don't get gigged." Don Jr. patted the front pocket of his overalls.

"I ain't afraid of you or your brother."

"Calm down now," Donald said. "Getting worked up over a bar whore."

"Tell Junior." Bobby looked at Donald. "Tell him it ain't right to say those things about Mary."

"What ain't right is choosing tail over money." Don Jr. stepped closer to Bobby Joe.

He flicked Bobby Joe with his middle finger, brushing his forehead like a pesky fruit fly, before skirting back to stand next to his brother.

Bobby Joe grunted and ground his teeth. Clenching both

fists, he stepped toward Don Jr., but Donald stopped him with his brass-knuckled hand on Bobby Joe's shoulder. "What my dimwitted brother's meaning to say is that you best think again before turning down this job."

Behind an old Dollar General a few miles south, he found the path the Brothers had described. He grabbed the black gym bag he used to store the stripped wire, and crabbed through the fence. Then he saw his moonlit shadow. A burly creature creeping into the deserted building. Thinking about what Donny Jr. had said about Mary, Bobby felt like a joke.

He was a criminal—and worse he was the kind of skunking around criminal who stole copper wire like a damned woman or a meth head.

Tossing the bag aside, Bobby headed back to the truck. He needed to warn Mary about the Donny Brothers, so he ran red lights as he headed for the camper parked behind Old Man Perkins' shotgun house. Perkins was like an uncle to Mary. He let her park her camper trailer in his backyard after her mamma got killed in a car wreck and her daddy was pulled for distribution. He gave her a job at the feed store, and even had his friend Bubba fix up one of his old beaters for her to drive around town.

Bobby pulled up to her camper, but saw there was no lights on. No car. As he stood outside his truck, with one hand on his truck door and the other on the steering wheel, he felt like the moon shined a spotlight down upon his lumberjack frame.

Mary was gone.

The thing about a really good woman is she makes you feel so good you forget to see the truth. He realized he'd let it get too complicated: Mary was more than a good lay. She made him forget the shit he'd been through. Her smile was his redemption. When he was with her, he felt like maybe he got a second chance, maybe the two of them could leave the shadows behind.

As he stood in the moonlight, he knew he'd been lying to himself for months. He let himself get caught.

The Donny Brothers would use Mary to keep him from

leaving the county. She might be his lighthouse, but she was also his anchor.

He stared inside one last time and saw everything scattered about the floor. A desk lamp broken, cups and plates shattered, picture frame busted into pieces, and clothes tossed about the bed.

He busted through the door and saw fresh blood in the debris. He sat on the edge of the bed and placed his head in his hands.

He knew, then, he should've fought like hell for Mary. She was a wild one, but he was the one at fault for kindling the flame. He kept just enough distance between them to make her feel she'd never be more than a good lay.

Sitting on the edge of her bed, crying, he knew Mary deserved a life outside of Indiana. She would have been better off if they never met.

Bobby Joe stopped crying longing enough to notice the broken picture frame beside of the night stand.

She was gone because of him.

As the early evening bled into midnight, Bobby Joe finally got up from the edge of the bed. He dried his face before making his way over Mary's debris and onto the metal trailer step. As his brown work boot touched gravel, the left side of his face was struck by brass knuckles. Blood poured out of his cheek. Bobby Joe, knocked to his knees, looked up and saw Don Jr. swing a bat wrapped in barbed toward his skull. The moon hovered behind him like a comic book cover.

Bobby Joe closed his eyes and fixed his thoughts on Mary.

Mary was long gone. She had borrowed Old Man Perkins' truck and hit the road just before sunset. Her eyes stretched out on the highway, a winding path through towns and cities that seemed to blur into one another.

Perkins had warned her Bobby Joe was in trouble, overheard it at the tavern. She'd exploded in a fit of rage and busted up just about everything she owned. She'd even punched the photo of her standing next to her mamma, cutting her skin along the broken glass. The frame was the only gift Bobby ever gave her.

A week later, Mary sat alone in a roadside bar just outside Memphis. She was low on cash and worried she'd need to make it to the next town on her back. She had cut and dyed her hair black. Her charcoal lipstick was smeared. She wore a torn V-neck with a Skynyrd logo on the front and tight, faded blue jeans. In one hand was a shot of tequila. In the other, a cold mug of beer.

Bobby Joe was a good man, but not worth losing her life over. Mary had convinced herself about that. Now she was lost because of him.

Mary pushed her empty mug away and was just about to head back to the truck, when two women, both curvy in black leather mini dresses, black fishnet stockings, and knee-high red stiletto boots, walked into the roadhouse accompanied by a man wearing eye shadow and dressed from head to toe in black leather. One of the women ordered ginger ale and the other woman gin and tonic. Aside from their slight height difference, the two could've been twins.

Mary couldn't help but ask, "Y'all in a stage show or something?"

The taller of the two began to play with the loose strands of her sun colored hair. She explained they were part of a religious country act that traveled the rural circuit, spreading their message of faith through music.

"I was a hooker," said the shorter of the two. "Went from one motel room to another hooked on pills."

"That there's Sherry, and my name's Jennifer," said the tall blonde. "I was into real estate back in the day. I was always dressing up in tight dresses selling city homes and commercial properties like it was dope."

Mary wrinkled her nose.

"The people I sold it to were just like the rednecks I knew from home," Jennifer explained, giggling and gently running her long, painted nails down Mary's arm. "They just wore expensive suits and could afford cocaine over meth."

Mary felt a connection because they confided in her so quickly. She felt a kinship that they weren't holy-rollers, just country gals that knew how to dress.

Just as Mary smiled at Jennifer, the man in eye shadow snuck himself between them.

"I'm Paul," he said, looking at Mary's V-neck as if he was trying to memorize the Skynyrd logo. "Bass player for the band."

His hair was dyed black, like Mary's. His nails were long and painted black. His lips glittered silver.

"You don't look religious," Mary said.

"Gospel is the Johnson Sisters' gig. They're true believers. I'm just in it for the tunes and the occasional smile from a girl like you."

"That was fucking lame." She turned away from Paul toward the sisters standing nearby, but they're having their own conversation.

Paul inched closer to Mary and farther from the sisters. His musky scent attracted her enough to look back. She licked her lips as his fingers traced the logo on the back pocket of her jeans.

"You've never heard me play the bass," he whispered. "These fingers can do God's work."

"That sounds much better than your earlier line," Mary admitted. "Maybe you can use those magic fingers to lead me out on the dance floor when the band starts their next set?"

"They can do more than that," he whispered, hooking four black-tipped fingers into her back pocket while his thumb trailed along the smooth flesh of her back.

Mary smiled, and over Paul's shoulder saw a baby-face man in a black cowboy hat and a red Nudie suit walking up to her. He smiled at Mary. Paul whispered into Mary's ear, "See you soon," and joined the sisters along the bar.

"I'm Daniel," the familiar looking man with the cowboy hat said. "I think we were neighbors once. You probably knew me as the preacher's son."

Mary looked around the barroom and back at Daniel.

"I don't remember you," she pretended. "I sure as hell don't remember any preacher's kid."

"You was with Old Man Perkins, right?"

"In a camper trailer out back," she corrected him.

"I grew up just down the road. We had the house near the church."

"Never went to church," she said.

"I know you," he said. "Seen you a time or two at the roadhouse. Always dancin', drinkin', and at times… shoutin' at someone."

Mary nodded. "Sounds like a typical Friday night. Tennessee's a long way to run into a hometown kid."

"I manage these folks," he said, nodding toward the three standing at the bar behind him. "We have other members that don't like to socialize as much. They're back at the hotel. Book gigs all around Appalachia."

"So you're just passing through Memphis?"

"Yep," he said, adjusting his cowboy hat. "We're on our way back from the Smokies to Kentucky. Playin' the Poke Sallet Fest up in Harlan."

"Ain't never been to Eastern Kentucky."

"What brings you to Tennessee?" he asked.

"Looking for something," she said.

"A job? We're in need of a road hand. Setting up equipment and whatnot. You can see the hills while you learn the ropes."

Mary fiddled with her hair. She looked over at Paul and thought of his fingers trailing along the curve of her back.

"I don't know," she said. "It sounds interesting, but I don't have experience with bands. I don't know anything about instruments."

"Nothing to it. I remember seeing you back home in the bar, always spitting fire. A tough girl that could hold her own. A smart one, too. We need that in our crew. We got electric tuners you can use… you'll pick up restringing in no time."

"Honestly, it sounds good," she said. "I've been so focused on today that I ain't thought much about tomorrow."

"That happens when we lose a loved one," he said.

"You knew my mamma?"

"I meant Bobby Joe," he said. "I figured that's why you're traveling on your own?"

Mary's brow furrowed. "What about Bobby Joe?"

"Old Man Perkins ran into my dad the other day," he said, looking down at his shiny boots. "Told him that the sheriff found Bobby Joe's truck near Hollows Ridge. Front end was so smashed it looked like it met both ends of a wrecking ball."

Mary closed her eyes.

"We called it quits before I left town," she lied. "I didn't know he was dead."

"They figure he hit the bank so hard he flew through the windshield and into the pit of Hollows Ridge."

"His body weren't in the truck?"

"Nope. They figure he's dead, though. Been gone all week. He weren't never one to leave town. My old man said there's talk about draining the pond to find his body."

She hugged him again.

"I always liked Bobby Joe," he said, letting her go. "I felt bad for what happened."

"What do you mean?"

"I was a mean kid… Aggressive one at that. I never should've hit him with a Bible."

"That was silly," she said, cracking a smile. "Why a Bible?"

"Bobby Joe kept saying Jesus was born from a hooker. He confused one Mary with another. He liked to tease me in those days. Saying, 'It was a hooker that created religion… because most men would believe anything for a good lay.'"

Mary laughed. "That does sound like Bobby Joe."

"Maybe he was onto something."

"You mean that heaven can be found between a woman's thighs?"

Daniel winked and said, "Don't let my old man hear of such truths. He'd be obliged to hire the likes of the Donny Brothers to keep folks believing."

Mary winced at the thought of the Donny Brothers.

"Bobby Joe would do anything for you," he said. "I'm sorry to be the one to tell you. I'm also sorry for losing my cool back in the day. Everyone always knew how quick-tempered Bobby Joe could be… I never should've provoked him. I wish I made the time to apologize."

"Maybe," she said. "But he never blamed nobody for something he did. No reason to dwell on it now. He's gone. I think we should always think of the good in Bobby Joe. Leave the rest of it behind."

"I think you're right," he said, lifting his cowboy hat and running his hand through his hair. "Since I was the one to tell you about his passing… maybe I could also be the one to give you a job?"

"As part of the crew?"

"The band could really use you as we head up to Harlan."

"When you leaving?"

"First thing tomorrow morning."

Mary nodded and said, "I'm in."

She turned from Daniel and walked closer to the edge of the bar. She ordered another shot of tequila and a cold mug of beer with the last few bills she had. She emptied the shot glass, slid it up the bar, and took a drink from the mug. She heard the band take the stage. The first song they played was "Don't Come Home A Drinking" followed by an old Hank Williams's standard, "My Love For You." She took another long drink from the mug and looked around the dim lit barroom for Paul.

Before her hips swayed to the steel guitar, and before Paul came over to reach out his long black-tipped fingers to lead her onto the dance floor, she drank from the cold mug. She drank until the last sip was gone.

Michael Amos Cody

"Carolina"

Asheville PD Detective Eddie Huntly stood with hat on and collar up against rain that fell cold and hard from the black sky above Deadman's Ridge. The late November storm's thunderous hiss thrummed on the body of the pickup parked on the shoulder behind him and the kayak upside down in its bed. Rain splashed on the two-lane blacktop underfoot. The din of the downpour hampered his hearing as effectively as the night obstructed his vision. But while intermittent flashes of lightning provided glimpses of the desolate surroundings, the thunder further hindered his ability to hear the approach of a danger that might destroy him as it had nearly done before—as it certainly had destroyed her—or slip past him and away, into Tennessee and a world beyond the grasp of his retribution. His chest tightened with fear and loss. Fear of his vulnerable position. Loss of the most desirable woman he'd ever held in his arms.

If his reason for being in that place at that moment was honorable, or at least by the book, he would be surrounded by backup, and the swirling blue lights would be glinting off drawn guns and glistening across POLICE rain gear and through the denuded woods. He would be listening to bloodhounds coming closer and driving his prey directly into his angry and aching embrace. But driven by blind passion, he stood devoid of reason, a lawless lawman and far gone from mercy. Stimulated by rage, he intended to terminate—to exterminate—his rival for lost Lily Davis's affections, to avenge her death by killing her killer.

A year before, she'd dropped from the window of a bedroom in her old daddy's house in Donegal, Pennsylvania, and made her way, suitcase in hand, along dark streets down to Jones Mill and Al Thorpe's room at the Log Cabin Lodge & Suites. The pair hit the road before sunup, with "Daddy Davis none the wiser," Huntly remembered Lily telling him one night. Driving a Ford Thunderbird and drinking Thunderbird wine, she and Thorpe took their time heading ever south: picnicking in parks alongside whitewater rivers, gawking at scenic overlooks, touring chilly caverns beneath the mountains, drinking and dancing and fighting in steamy taverns every night, and fucking whenever Thorpe wanted it. Finally coming to rest on the Swannanoa edge of Black Mountain, they rented an isolated mobile home in a deep holler that daily received less than five hours of direct sunlight—when there was any to be had. He got a job with Waste Pro and rode the back of a garbage truck five days a week while she sat alone in the quiet of their holler.

She'd overwintered with Thorpe, sending a Christmas card to her daddy in Donegal, postmarked Asheville but without return address. That mild winter passed with little of either snow or sunshine—only inches and inches of rain. By the end of a stormy lion-lion March, she'd had enough of his beer farts and butt slaps, his bad horror movies and pay-per-view MMA nights, and the sleepwalking that tended to end with him outside in the rain wearing nothing but his yellowing drawers or with his ham hands fumbling at her body from toes to throat.

So, on an April new-moon night without rain, she left him a note: "Thanks for the ride down from Pa. I'm getting myself out of reach of your hard hands that smell like other people's garbage." Before she lay down the pencil, she added, "P.S. I might be back, and I might not." She slipped outside and made her way, suitcase in hand, down the holler to North Fork Road, where she caught a ride into Asheville, arriving just at sunrise—a hopeful sign, she thought.

But sunset found her standing on the corner of Lexington and Hiawassee, hungry and aching from the bottom of her feet to the top of her head and trying to swallow the fear that one of the next vehicles would screech to a stop and Thorpe would sit glaring at her from behind the wheel. Eventually, a man—not

Thorpe—stopped, and without letting herself think about it, she'd fucked him and received for her troubles his money and then a hard slap across the face as confusing as Thorpe's somnambulistic violence.

The seventh man in that first week away from the Black Mountain holler gave her not only elaborate praise for her skin and curves and more compensation than they'd settled on but also a sympathetic ear. Then he drove her east, back into Swannanoa, and by lunchtime the next day, she'd moved into a two-bedroom apartment already housing three other young women about her age. After a few days' rest to recover her glow, learn some basic maneuvers up and down and around the pole, and put together her first display, she found herself employed, like her roommates, as an untouchable dancer at the Treasure Club, one of the dozen referenced on the sign by the road—"12 PRETTY GIRLS; 1 UGLY ONE."

Detective Huntly pulled his collar tighter against the rain and shuddered at both the chill of a rainy night on Deadman's Ridge and the memory of the first time he saw "Carolina Lily," the name she'd chosen for the stage. He'd never felt drawn to places like the Treasure Club and had come that time only at the insistence of a colleague who believed a serial burglary-and-assault suspect might be found there. After waiting almost an hour, standing at the back of a bloat of middle-aged men with out-of-style eyeglasses and fixated stares, neither colleague nor suspect in sight, he stepped to the bar to close out his tab. He heard her introduced over a club-mix of "Take Me to Church," and when he turned from the bar toward the door, he stopped, suddenly unsteady as he watched her go around and around the Treasure Club's pole in a dizzying—for him, at least—Juliet Spin. The throbbing red velvet world disappeared, leaving only the swirling beauty of her.

By the end of that first night, he'd paid seventy-five dollars for three lap dances in a darkened room with intimate, private booths, and he drove home with her fragrance—something of honeysuckle and patchouli—in his clothes. By the end of a second night, he left with her fragrance—her scent—not only on his clothes but also on his fingers and lips. At the end of the third night, he drove home with her scent—a delicious aroma—enveloping him, radiating from her as she sat in the passenger seat, a warm hand on his thigh.

Some weeks after that night, the first evening when neither was working, they sat in bathrobes at his kitchen table and ate pizza from Del Vecchio's with Cold Mountain from Highland.

"You want me to quit?" she said.

"Do you want to quit?"

She turned up the amber bottle and drained the remainder of her beer, set the bottle down and released a small, airy burp. "Most of the time, I like what I'm doing. The dancing—"

"You've got a great body for it," he said. "And for more than just dancing."

She didn't smile as he expected. Instead, she shivered and pulled the robe tighter around herself, and he wondered if he should have said something else.

"There's a man," she said.

"What man?"

Then she told him her story, although he hadn't asked—had never asked. How she'd used a man named Al Thorpe as her ticket out of Donegal, PA. How they'd wound up in Black Mountain and she'd tried to learn to love the man—in spite of his drinking, his jealousies, his fixation on violence, his volatile sleepwalking—until she was too afraid to try any longer. How she'd left him alone in the middle of one dark night and found herself likewise alone and in need on Lexington Avenue. How for a week she'd bartered with seven different men for the brief use of her body until the last set her up with roommates who became coworkers at her Treasure Club gig. How ever since she left that Black Mountain holler, she'd been looking over her shoulder for a coming reckoning with Thorpe. She'd seen him just the morning before at the apartment complex, riding the back of a garbage truck.

"He looked straight at my window," she said and stopped.

Huntly nodded and lifted the last slice of pizza from the box. He offered it to her with a gesture and a raised eyebrow, and when she shook her head, he let it slump onto his plate. He hadn't told her he was a detective, and since she hadn't asked, he figured she'd grown used to such discrete omissions from the men she met. After his first night at the club, he'd driven his Honda Ridgeline so she wouldn't see the truth his gadget-filled undercover car told—and maybe so her scent wouldn't perfume the interior and linger well into the next day for his partner to sniff. His spartan apartment told no tales, keeping his secret in the closet, hanging with his ceremonial dress blues.

He pushed back his chair, stood with open robe, and held out his hand. "We don't need to worry about him," he said. "One more round before I run you home?"

Al Thorpe had woken up alone that morning after Lily Davis disappeared, winced at the note she'd left, and then spent several days under the weight of a confused silence, hanging on to the back of his Waste Pro truck and speaking little to the men he worked with. He felt light-headed each time he returned to the holler, expecting she might be waiting there for him with an apology on her lips and between her thighs. Unable to sleep in the bed he'd shared with her, he slept fitfully in a chair in front of the TV and woke up some mornings with mud on his feet or keys in his hand. His pain eventually swelled to rage and drove him out of his solitude to the streets of Asheville, where, during most of the hours between getting off work and going back, he drank and fought and fucked his way to scraps of information amounting to little more than that a young woman matching Lily's description had been in the Lexington Avenue area for a week or so before he showed up and that nobody had seen her the previous night or two. Finally, in a downtown motel room, the last woman he hired pointed him in the direction of the Treasure Club before she laughed at his obsession with such an inexperienced girl.

Thorpe had left her bloodied and bruised and owing the room bill, retreated to his holler, and slept away the weekend. Monday morning broke bright with sunshine and found him clear-headed. He went to work thinking that he wouldn't bring Lily back to the same life she'd fled. He would find a better job and a better place and be a better man—all for her. Every evening he bought a box of Kentucky Fried Chicken and a sixpack of Budweiser and parked in the farthest corner of the Treasure Club lot. From there he watched her arrive, but for the longest time he couldn't bring himself to go in to see what she did in the pulsing darkness beyond the club's front door. So, every night, after finishing his beers, he fell asleep behind the wheel and later awoke alone in the lot.

One Monday evening he arrived late without chicken or beer and found the spaces around him packed with what appeared to him to be twice as many vehicles as was normal even for a weekend night. Curious and figuring he could easily hide in the midst of such a crowd, he left his vehicle and headed for the door, at the last moment attaching himself to the rear of a party of six or seven young women and men. He'd never been inside, but he imagined that it wouldn't be much different from the dozens of similar places he'd spent time and money in between Florida and Pennsylvania. Yet even before he followed the group through the door, he realized how wrong such imagining was. This, he thought, would be vastly different because Lily was inside.

Then she wasn't.

Music throbbed as he paid his cover charge, and people talked loudly and moved in silhouette. But the pole he expected to see gleaming at the center of the darkness was absent. The stage had been caged, its floor padded, and two men fought furiously and awkwardly in unforgiving spotlights. One was a thinly muscled man dressed out in the finest MMA gear Walmart had on offer, the other a shirtless jelly doughnut in blue jeans and bare feet.

Al Thorpe's bloodlust liquefied his brain before the door closed behind him, washing away his longing for Lily and causing his hand to shake so that he could barely sign up for his turn in the cage.

Some three hours later, he lurched zombielike—with skinned knuckles, bruised body, and rattled brain—back to his lonely holler and squeezed into a tub of stinging Epsom salts, the bathroom floor papered with sodden prizemoney.

When Lily locked her Closed Rainbow—the most advanced position she'd achieved, already a favorite with the regulars—and opened her eyes to take in an upside-down view of the crowd on Public Service Night, the shock of seeing both Eddie Huntly and Al Thorpe in the room at the same time almost caused her to lose the knee grip she had on the pole.

Each stood with a small cluster of other men at opposite ends of the back wall. Each fixated on her with stares only slightly more intense than those of the men surrounding them.

As "Wicked Game" moved into its second chorus, she released the Closed Rainbow and moved into the second half of her routine. Although she couldn't allow any random gazer—"client"—in the crowd to suspect she wasn't on display for him alone, she couldn't but be aware of those particular two unwittingly vying for possession of her.

As the third verse progressed, she worked through a series of simpler maneuvers that became more poses than positions, slowing her transitions between these and lingering with them in the way she knew the eyes in the room liked best. By midway through the final choruses, she transitioned downward with the crowd favorite Back Slide Wide Leg.

Movement just beyond the lights broke her fragile concentration, and she released the seductive nibble on her lower lip as her eyes flared wide at the sight of big Al Thorpe lumbering toward her, shoving his way through the startled men that had served as a barrier between her and him.

Distracted by the inexplicable appearance—on Public Service Night no less—of the serial burglary-and-assault suspect he'd been seeking, Huntly didn't register Thorpe's charge toward Lily until the big man was already clambering over the lip of the stage. He broke from the formation moving to surround the newly arrived suspect as Thorpe lifted a screaming Lily by her wrist. Huntly pushed through the crowd of men rising to their feet, and when they seemed to clear a runway for him, he leapt to the stage just as Thorpe—with Lily in hand—began to turn.

As if in command of some preternatural sense of his surroundings, or as if the three of them had rehearsed this a dozen times, Thorpe spun counterclockwise and behind his back switched his grip on Lily's wrist from his right hand to his left. As he continued the spin, his freed right hand shot out and cupped the back of Huntly's head. With the combined momentums of the lawman's running jump and his own spin, Thorpe slammed Huntly's forehead into the shining silver pole like a "heel" slamming a "face" into a turnbuckle. Huntly's body locked in spasm for a fraction of a second and then crumpled to the stage. Thorpe released Lily and dropped atop the downed lawman, straddling him, and rained down a fury of hammer-fisted blows.

The last things Huntly remembered were the creature rage in Thorpe's eyes, the blurry movement of bouncers and fellow officers bodily lifting the maniac off of him, and Lily screaming, "You're police? Eddie? Fucking police?"

Less than eighteen seconds of stunning brutality landed him in the hospital for two days.

Amid the pandemonium of frightened men hiding their faces and fumbling toward the exits, the shrill cacophony of screams from Lily and the other dancers, and frantic ministrations to the broken detective, Al Thorpe escaped. He hid in his rainy holler for a day and packed to leave the Asheville area with his freedom, his pride, and his girl. He gathered the few bags that held his clothes and those Lily had left and placed them by the front door. Then he settled down in his chair to sleep a few hours before their getaway.

In a dream, he threw everything into the bed of a pickup he didn't recognize and abandoned both mobile home and waterlogged holler. He passed through the door of the Treasure Club and found Lily. Somehow he couldn't get to her as she wound herself around the pole in ways physically impossible and impossibly high, ways that raised in him an aching desire. That policeman—Eddie was the name she'd screamed—lay still at the foot of her pole, but as he watched, the man began to stir and rise and then to shinny up the shining shaft toward Lily. Whatever held him back fell away, and he struggled forward through shifting and tumbling tables and chairs. At last, he flopped onto the stage and lurched up and pulled the man down. Then he was once more astraddle his foe—the two of them somehow suddenly naked—with his hands wrapped tightly around the lawman's pulsing neck. Above, Lily screamed and laughed and screamed as Eddie's eyes fixed on nothing and his pathetic resistance fell away.

Thorpe's eyelids fluttered open to find the windows framing morning light and himself sitting naked and chilled in his chair. He leaned forward and sat a few breaths with elbows on knees and face in hands smelling of honeysuckle and patchouli. After a vigorous rubbing of sleep from his eyes while distorted images of the dream flashed through his mind like madness, he stood to look for his clothes. Not finding them and thinking he must have shed them outside in the muddy grass, he dug in his bags for dry underwear, t-shirt, and jeans. Then he pulled on socks and shoes and hoisted all his stuff and hers. With hands too full to close the door behind himself, he left it standing open, stowed the bags in the Thunderbird, and skidded out of their holler.

By the time Detective Eddie Huntly was being discharged from Mission Hospital, his colleagues had learned all they could about his raging attacker and strategized a raid on Thorpe's house trailer.

Detective Shawn Hendricks picked him up outside the hospital. "Damn, son, you sure you're up for this?" he said when Huntly opened the cruiser's passenger door.

"I'm fine," Huntly said, fell into the seat, and slammed the door. "Looks worse than it feels."

"I'm pretty sure that's bullshit," Hendricks said.

"Drive," Huntly said and dialed Lily's number, but the call went straight to voicemail.

With no vehicle in the yard and the trailer's door standing open, Huntly figured Thorpe was already in the wind and a clear and present danger to Lily. Still, he went inside the place where she'd spent the past winter with that monster. While most of the uniformed officers and detectives rolled out of the holler and Hendricks sat in the car and set BOLOs in motion, Huntly cleared and searched the trailer.

He found her body in the bedroom at the end of the hall, where she lay on her back, mostly covered but cold to the touch, her neck ringed with bruising and her eyes open and seemingly fixed on the rain thrumming the roof.

Huntly sat rigid at his desk, stone-faced and staring at his telephone. The moment it rang, his left hand shot out and yanked up the receiver.

"Bet you want a piece of me, Eddie," a gruff voice said.

"God damn you," Huntly said.

"Tell me when and where"—Thorpe made a noise, something

between a groan and a growl—"and I'll finish beating the fucking life out of you."

Detective Huntly holstered his sidearm and rubbed the lullaby of rain and strain of staring from his eyes. When his hands came away from his face, Al Thorpe stood not ten feet away, hunched and panting on the down-ridge edge of the blacktop. Huntly drew his gun again and leveled it at Thorpe's open mouth.

The big man steadied his breathing and stood straight, staring past the barrel into Huntly's eyes. "Thought we was finishing this man to man," he said.

"You're no man."

A sweet and familiar scent passed like a breeze between them. Huntly felt the jolt of it in his skull and chest and loins, and he saw that Thorpe felt it, too. Thorpe's shoulders slumped, and Huntly's aim dropped to the big man's gut.

"I sleepwalk," Thorpe said, his voice husky and almost plaintive. "I didn't even know—" He stopped. Then, when Huntly again raised the barrel to his face, "I didn't know."

"Bullshit." The rain intensified, and Huntly felt cold drops drip from the brim of his hat and slide down his back. Dim as the lonely place was, he could see drops dangling from Thorpe's earlobes and the blunt end of his nose.

The sweet scent of honeysuckle and patchouli now hovered between them as if Lily herself stood there separating them like a referee in a wrestling ring.

Scent and image stung Huntly's eyes.

Thorpe charged, and Huntly fired.

The big man's powerful body crashed into the lawman, and Huntly felt a rib crack as he fell with Thorpe on his chest and his back to the blacktop. He tried to work himself from underneath the monster before ham hands could wrap around his throat. But he quickly realized that Thorpe wasn't wrestling with him, just dead weight that moved only when he moved.

Huntly stilled, and for a moment the two lay cheek to cheek in the road as rain fell.

After a few pained breaths, he managed to roll Thorpe's body from on top of him. He stood and wiped blood from his lips and looked down at the bullet hole in the forehead and eyes staring unseeing into the dark and weeping sky.

Gasping, wincing, spitting, sometimes crying aloud, Huntly worked Thorpe's body back to the down-ridge edge of the blacktop and then pushed it over the side. He remained on his knees, moving only enough to find those temporary positions that pained him least. He stared downward through woods he couldn't see into farther than fifteen feet, toward the river he couldn't see at all. When headlights crossed Wilson's Bridge and seemed to slow for the right turn that would bring him unwanted company, he rose with a groan and stumbled to his truck.

He dropped off Deadman's Ridge and took Highway 251 north along the French Broad through Marshall. Between Runion and Hot Springs, he maneuvered his truck down an overgrown river access. After removing his license tag and flinging it toward the dark hulk of Mountain Island, he wrestled the kayak out of the bed of the truck and into the river, hoping to reach Tennessee before daybreak.

Ron Cooper

"Wild Wind"

Mary left Dr. Skinner's office as Good Time Charlie was entering. "Hey, Charlie," she said.

"Hey, Ms. Mary. I reckon you heard about Lefty."

"What?"

"He got into some kind of mess at the feed store yesterday and got took in, I believe."

She shook her head. "Not surprised. Wonder what he was doing at the feed store."

Wandering Bill leaned against the wall outside the doctor's office.

"Charlie won't let you go in with him Bill?"

"He ain't my boss, Ms. Mary. He here for a 'scription. I can't stand me no doctor office. They smell scary to me."

Mary crossed Main Street to Luther Martin's news stand.

"Hey, Ms. Too Tall," Luther said. An open bottle of MD 2020 sat on the table beside him.

"Let me get a copy of *The Register*," Mary said. "I hear Lefty got arrested again."

"It's right there on the front page. Anything like that is big news around here." Luther took a swig of his wine and wiped his mouth with the back of his hand. "Probably make you happy, y'all being divorced and all."

Mary read the first two paragraphs of the story in silence. "Me and that asshole don't talk with one another. I'm just wondering what it's all about and how he got his ass out of county without asking me to go his bail." She read a little more. "Huh. Says here he was buying horse feed. He can't afford no horse."

Luther pointed to the street. "Ask him. Yonder he goes."

Mary turned around to see a shiny new red Ford F-250 passing by. "What the holy goddamnit hell? He can't afford no brand new truck, not on disability. Last I heard he might've even lost that." Luther extended his arm and waved his hand to wipe along the street. "Was a time when I could've had a truck like that. You know my family used to own about all these businesses here."

"We all know that, Luther."

"Look at me now. Selling papers, drinking cheap-ass wine. Living in my family's run-down old house, even if it's a big'un. Roof leaks. The whole thing needs painted. Might be bats in the attic. If I had a big old pile of money in the bank like you I'd fix it up and rent out some rooms."

"Everybody knows about you Luther, but bank? You know I hate banks! Hell, they nearly about ruint my daddy just like they did yours. You know that." Mary folded the paper and tucked it under her arm. "Don't you worry, Luther. You going to be all right. That's the way it goes around here."

Good Time Charlie exited Dr. Skinner's office. "Give me a cigarette."

Wandering Bill reached into his hoody pocket and pulled out a Timeless Time. "Last one. How much you get?"

Charlie lit the cigarette with a butane lighter with "Don't Mess with Texas" stamped on it. "None. Son of a bitch done doubled his price. Said his risk is bigger."

"What we gonna do? Ain't us neither one can go without some of them pills."

"I'm already thinking a plan I got about," said Charlie. "How big your balls feeling today?"

Bill mounted his spider bicycle. "Big enough. I'm up for what in the hell ever you got."

Charlie pointed his chin down Main Street. "You be back over on the corner up from Hoppy's Drive In at seven. I got an idea. Wear a hoodie. Bring a handkerchief."

"What you got in mind?"

"Just do like I say. Don't tell a damn soul where you going."

Mary entered her house and looked around for strength. The big room, as she called it, was filled with mid-century furniture, most of it in cracked plastic covers. Much of the pale blue paint on the walls was pealing. A finely painted portrait of her paternal grandparents adorned with formal attire, her grandmother cuddling a spaniel, hung over the fireplace that had not been lit in years. On the wall opposite the Main Street window on a narrow shelf leaned a framed photograph from a Brownie camera of her maternal grandparents, her grandfather as always in overalls and flannel shirt and her grandmother in her gingham dress and blue apron with white stripes. In the background was the barn that she remembered homed two or three cows and a mule. What would they all expect of her?

She hurried upstairs to her bedroom. The bedsheets and slips on the chairs were old but not yellowed. Upon the top drawer of her white dresser sat three jewel boxes. Each held what she had been told was antique jewelry from her paternal grandmother and her great-grandmother. She opened the boxes and found everything intact. She then pulled out the bottom drawer, closed her eyes, whispered the Lord's Prayer, and removed an oversized Bible and set it atop the dresser beside the picture of her paternal grandfather shaking hands with Lyndon Johnson.

Some pages in, about Exodus or Isaiah, she never could remember, she found the rectangular hole cut into the lower pages.

The hole was empty.

She poured a glass of Beefeater from the finely cut crystal bottle by the picture of her college graduation. She thought for a moment of her degree in European history and how much of it was a study of deceit and murder.

"That bastard finally robbed me," she mumbled. She toasted herself in her reflection of the dresser mirror.

Hoppy closed at six PM even on the weekends and refused anyone who banged at the door a minute later. He did good business, and his life did not depend upon barefoot stragglers who couldn't afford a watch. He spent a few minutes afterwards getting things in order for the next day before heading home for supper with Eugenie and a bit of TV. Friday was his night to do some extra cleaning and stacking in the back room, and he turned off the lights in the front to signify further that he was indeed closed.

Like most other business owners on Main Street he had only a simple lock on the front door knob—no dead bolt, no alarm system. In this tiny town crimes consisted of drunken domestic violence, drunken kids stealing cars for joyrides around the county, or drunken idiots in brawls like Lefty had started at the feed store. All were acts of utmost stupidity, since everybody knew each other and had no chance to get away with their ill-formed schemes. The only break-in in the past five years was when Tash Gilbey had jiggled open the door to Hamby's Hardware two years ago and was found passed out drunk the next morning by the cash register with a set of drill bits in his hand.

A soft rattling sound came from the store front. Hoppy paid it no mind. The wind was picking up, so it was probably just the loose window pane by the door. Then he heard the chime of the bell that hung over the door.

He stepped toward the front. "We're closed."

Two slim figures stood inside. "We know," said one. They were both in dark hoodies and with handkerchiefs over the bottoms of their faces.

Hoppy leaned over the counter. "What the hell y'all think y'all doing? You think I got any money here?"

"Give us what you got in the register," one said.

Hoppy reached under the counter. "The hell I will. Goddammit, is that you, Bill?"

One of the hooded intruders stepped towards Hoppy. "Just give us the money, old man."

The shotgun erupted, and the robber crumpled to the ground. The other intruder squealed and escaped out the front door.

"I'm sorry, son," said Hoppy. "What the hell did you expect? That's the way it goes."

Mary drove around town in her old Oldsmobile 88. She found Luther Martin walking towards the VFW. She slowed and rolled down the front passenger window.

"Luther, what you doing walking out here at night?"

Luther pointed to a sheet of paper in his hand. "I can't remember ever seeing you out driving, Ms. Too Tall. Anyway, big dance tonight. Band from way out of town like Beaumont or Waco."

"You know those are way off different parts of the state, right? Anyway, I never known you to go to a dance."

"I never been to one. I probably won't dance. Don't nobody want to dance with me no way. Just thought I might hear some good music. I hope nobody don't mind me. Don't even know if I got enough money for a ticket."

"Don't worry about that. Hop in. I'll give you a ride."

Luther climbed into the front passenger seat. "I ain't never known you to drive your car. I had one, I'd head out to somewhere—maybe Beaumont or Waco. Hell, I ain't never been nowhere. About anywhere else even in Texas, might as well be Kalamazoo to me."

As they neared the parking lot, they passed Good Time Charlie on his banana seat bike peddling as fast as he could.

"I reckon he going to the dance, too," Luther said.

"I kind've doubt that," said Mary. "You ever seen him at any community function?"

"I don't know about no community function, but I reckon not."

Behind them towards the center of town they heard a police siren.

"Wonder what's going on back yonder?" Luther asked.

Mary chuckled. "What all could it be around here? Some drunk ass started some shit in the pool hall or ran into a stop sign."

They stopped in the parking lot. Mary pointed to a truck. "Luther, don't that look like the truck what we saw Lefty in today?"

"It sure do, Ms. Too Tall. I ain't seen none other like that one around."

Mary handed Luther some bills. "Here. That ought to be enough to get you in and buy yourself a few drinks. Find yourself a pretty girl to dance with."

"I don't know about that, Ms. Too Tall, but you about the best friend I got."

"Hush up, Luther."

Mary parked behind the red Ford truck. She left her car and approached Charlie who sat at the far edge of the parking lot by a gum tree with his bike laid on the ground beside him. As she got near, Charlie tried to hide behind the tree.

"I seen you Charlie. Come here. I need to talk to you."

Charlie crawled out low, as if expecting gunfire.

"What kind of trouble you in, Charlie?" she asked. "You know me. Level with me."

"I'm in big, big trouble, Ms. Mary. I got to get out of here."

"How big?"

"Just believe me. Enough to get my ass in the pen. I got to get out of here, but I ain't got no money and no car."

"And no pills neither, right?"

"Yes'm. I ain't never been this deep in anything. I'm sorry. I done said too much." He picked up his bike.

Police sirens sounded again.

"Hold up," Mary said. She put her hands into her jeans back pockets, turned around and looked up. In the night sky she saw the Little Dipper and followed it out to see Polaris. "I might be able to help you."

"I don't want you involved in this. I should just get out of here."

Mary spun back around. "Shut the fuck up. I'm thinking them sirens have something to do with you, right? If you want to get out of here, you'll listen to me, got it? Now I'm going to go into the VFW. If I come out with Lefty—you know him, my first ex-husband, right?—and we get into that new red Ford truck in front of my car, you follow us in my car wherever we go. You can drive, right?"

"Yes'm. I got a license."

"OK. Then you do what I tell you."

"Yes'm."

Downstairs in the crowded dance hall Mary found nearly half the town. A band in the corner played Otis Redding's "Fa-Fa-Fa" song, and everyone was singing along. Her high school friends Dan and Margarita were close-dancing together. Mary thought they'd split up, but it looked like they had made up or were trying to. Even the old men shooting pool were singing. In the middle of the floor with a space created around them by the others a couple slid and spun around with exceptional grace. It was old Doc Skinner and Beatrice Goolsby. Doc Skinner was the best dancer in town with moves that made everyone think of TV cloggers on old country music shows, high-stepping and twisting as if he were part buck-dancer and part ballet leaper. No one could come close to his style. Some wondered if he'd missed his calling as a professional jazz footer, but they were happier that he was their medicinal caretaker.

From the staircase where she'd stopped Mary saw her second ex-husband Julius. He was looking into his dungaree pocket and grinning as if he'd found a treasure. He looked at her with a long pause, and although she grinned, she shifted her gaze hoping he hadn't noticed. Even in his raggy leather jacket and battered brogans he was as good looking as she remembered.

Leaning unsteadily against the bar, no surprise, was Lefty.

She crossed the room around the dancers and near the wall nodding to but speaking to no one. She sidled up beside Lefty and ordered a gin and tonic.

"Well, look who's here," slurred Lefty. Mary could tell by his watery, red eyes he was deep into his drink. "Ain't seen you in a coon's age. Since when you come to… come to these dances?"

Mary did not meet his gaze. "Heard you had some trouble yesterday."

Lefty huffed. "Just a misunderstanding. You know how Carlos always trying to pull something, some shit."

"Whatever." Mary gulped down her drink. "Say, how about you and me take a ride. We ain't spent any time together in a good while."

"How you mean?"

She set down her glass and waved for another. "No sense in not being friends. Hell, this is a small town. Ain't you tired of us trying to avoid each other? Beside, I see you got a sweet new ride."

"What, you saying want to take, take a spin with me?"

"I just feel like we got unfinished business, don't you? That way we can get on with our lives."

"All right, then. Let me get another, a drink for the, you know, for the road."

"Don't worry about that." Mary held up a flask, winked, and finished her drink. "Let's go out to the old boat landing wash out where we can have some private time together."

Lefty pinched Mary's elbow. "I can go for that."

Lefty parked facing the creek where the full moon shone over the trees swaying in the wind.

"Wild wind coming in tonight," said Mary. "I love watching the trees bending over, don't you?" She pulled a leather encased flask from her pocketbook. Her initials were tooled into it along with a scene of hunters and bird dogs. "Have a swig of this. It's the most expensive stuff you can get. Pappy Van Winkle, but I just don't see the big deal about it."

"I've been wanting to, to try of it, you know, for a hell of a while." Lefty took a long pull. "Not bad, but it got a, a strange after you, how you say, aftertaste. I still like it pretty good, though. Damn!"

"Have another swallow," Mary said. "I brought it just for you. I know how you like your good bourbon, but I reckon you ain't able to afford it lately."

He took another pull from the flask. "How you know what I can't afford? You in my new truck, ain't you?'

"I've been wondering about that. You got a new job or something?"

"You don't need to be in my business." Lefty handed the flask back to her. "That's a damn bigass flask. Must be from your mama."

"Don't you remember that I'm not a bourbon woman? Anyways, I drank enough back at the hall. Let's just enjoy this nice view for a little bit."

They sat in silence for ten minutes.

Lefty pointed to the rear view mirror. "Some damn body done pulled up behind of us."

"Just some kids," Mary said. "This a big parking spot for teenagers. Have another swallow. We can just enjoy the windy night and then I want to talk to you."

"Whatever."

Minutes later Lefty rubbed his forehead. "Damn. That must've been some strong ass, Jesus, whiskey you give me. Hell, I'm feeling, I'm feel woozy as shit."

"You sure?"

"What you call, call that, that, damn, that, hell."

"Finish, it up, Lefty. I promise you'll feel better."

Lefty upended the flask, and gagged. "They's some, some grit or shit, shit in the bot, bottom it." He tossed the flask onto the floorboard.

"How you feeling?"

"Not too, too," Lefty's head fell sideways against the window. "Where we gone, at where we?"

Mary touched his shoulder. "Listen to me, you bastard. I done loaded your ass up with oxy, ground into that whiskey. I know you stole my money, you son of a bitch. You done spent a heap of it on your bail and this damn truck, but where is the rest? Tell me now, or I'll fucking gut you like a fish right here."

Lefty raised his right hand as if swearing. "OK. You, you, you. It here. I did. It here. Help. I did. Help me." His head slid down the window.

"Here?" Mary opened the glove box. She found a .38 Smith & Wesson revolver and papers for the purchase of the truck. She then opened the console between the seats. Underneath several receipts from fast food restaurants, napkins, and a pair of reading glasses, she found a stack of bills. She flipped through them for a moment—it looked like at least 40,000 dollars.

"You bastard. I knew you robbed me. Now it's your sorry goddamn ass."

Mary and Charlie pushed the Ford F-250 into the creek.

"You think it's going to go under, Ms. Mary?"

Mary kicked her shoes together and spat on the mud. "Got to. That creek's full of vehicles and bodies. One more don't mean nothing."

The truck sank to the top of the doors.

"Fuck," Mary said. "We might have to wade out there and push some more."

Just then the truck went completely under the water.

Charlie clapped his hands and hopped. "Whoowee! Lefty done gone!"

"Settle down, Charlie. Here's what's going to happen. You listening?"

"Yes, ma'am."

"You're going to drive me home. I'm going to give you some

money, and you're going to leave town with my car. Ditch the car way off somewhere. Oklahoma, Arkansas, wherever. Everybody knows I almost never drove it and kept it in the garage behind the house, so there won't be any question for awhile about my missing car. Here, take Lefty's wallet. The driver's license picture don't look a whole lot like you, but people at hotels or wherever don't look too close. You should be able to get pretty far away before anything happens. You hear me?"

Back into town, she had him stop at Luther Martin's house. "Wait right here, Charlie."

Luther came to the door.

"You back from the dance already, Luther?"

"I'm sorry. I went in for a minute or two, but you know I get nervous."

"Take this," she said. "It's a good heap of money. You can fix your roof and then take a trip to Waco or Beaumont. You can just never, ever, tell anyone where you got the money. You got that?"

"Why you giving me this, Ms. Too Tall?"

"Shut up, Luther. Just take it, OK? Didn't you say I was the only friend you had? Don't friends do things for friends? Like I said, don't tell nobody where you got the money. They'll all just think it was an inheritance that you've been keeping back."

"I think I might just go to Waco. Shoot, maybe even New Orleans!"

"You do that, Luther. Have some real fun for once."

Charlie stopped the car at Mary's house.

"Here," she said. "This is about twenty thousand dollars. It ought to get you a good ways out of here. You didn't kill nobody, right?"

"No ma'am, nothing like that, but here's the thing. Doc Skinner raised his prices, so me and Bill tried to hold up Old Hoppy. We thought Hoppy was gone, but he jumped up and shot Bill. I don't know how bad off Bill was, but I ran. I'm so damn scared."

"So that's what the sirens were."

"Yes'm. I'm so worried about Bill."

Mary backhanded Charlie across his face. "You stupid ass! What the hell were you thinking? Everybody knows you and Bill were inseparable, goddamn asshole buddies, so they'll be looking for you whatever shape Bill's in. I swear, this town is just filled with dumbasses. But don't worry about Bill. Hoppy just keeps a .410 loaded with bird shot under his counter."

Charlie sobbed.

Mary put her hand on Charlie's shoulder. "Listen. You can still get away. Just remember that the most they have on you is attempted robbery, and that ain't much. Hell, Hoppy might get the worst of it. If they somehow track you down, you have to admit to the attempted robbery, understand? But you know nothing about Lefty. Got it?"

"Yes, ma'am."

"You sure? Got it?"

The wind had picked up and was howling.

Mary lit a Lucky Strike. "You know I'll never admit to anything about Lefty if that ever comes up. I'll say that Lefty and I went for a drive, then he brought me back to the VFW where I got my car and drove home. None of those drunk asses at the dance will know any better. They'll have nothing on me. Nobody'll miss Lefty for weeks, and if they do, they'll have no reason to suspect me. If they ask about my car, I'll just say that I drive it so rarely I don't even know when it went missing. So you're on your own now, right?"

"I thank you. Ms. Mary." Charlie wiped his face. "One more thing. You got any pills? Doc Skinner wouldn't sell me any today."

Mary leaned her head back and sighed. "Goddamnit." She reached into her pocketbook and pulled out several oxycontin pills. "Just don't take these while you're driving, you dumbass. Got it? You got to keep your cool and not wreck."

"Yes'm. Thank you."

Mary opened the car door. "Now I'm going in, and I'm going to sleep like a baby. You put some miles between here and wherever the hell else, maybe Waco. Maybe Tulsa. Just don't throw that money around and raise suspicions. Okay?"

"Yes'm."

"You hear me?"

"Yes'm." Charlie rubbed his eyes. "One last thing. Everybody knows you had a heap of family money. Why'd you never spend it on anything?"

Mary took a final drag on her cigarette and flipped the butt out onto her yard. "Had? I still got some. I'm thinking about doing like you and heading out for a new life." She stepped out of the car. "Feel that wild wind? It sure blows."

Sandra Johnson Cooper

"The Road Goes on Forever"

For about the fifteenth fucking time, Sheri berated herself because just what in the hell had possessed her to follow that bitch out to his Blazer. She couldn't even fake being kidnapped because that asshole Scooter had pulled the most godawful smirk when she ran after Sonny. Why wouldn't he be smirking; afterall, how many times had she made fun of Son. She laughed at everything about him: the stupid fucking ass cowboy hat and boots he wore (for god's sake, they were in fucking SC—if he had to wear a hat, Gandalf, blend in with a baseball cap), to his failing the fucking ASVAB. So, she knew she was going to catch hell skinking back into her shift Friday night, and she already knew she would be skinking back because, like it or not, she made good tips. These Friday-rich fuckers cash their paychecks before they come to town, and the place turns into "Wooden Horses": the axles of the F150s burning the road up to get the fat trailer tots and lint-heads up in here to play twangy ass trash country about watermelons and sweet tea while they order variations of draft beer until the beer goggles get thick enough for them to go home in twos and threesomes. As far as she was concerned, they were all getting the short ends of the ugly sticks. The job was pretty easy because whatever draft they ordered—and they all ordered draft—she just brought them PBR, and not a one of them with their refined sensibilities noticed. As long as she showed up, JC allowed her to cultivate her own garden. It might not be Eldorado, but at least she didn't work out in the weather.

Anyway, she was in the duct taped front seat of this goddamned rusted Blazer because Son had gone all Sir Lancelot, and she had Guinevered all over herself. She couldn't even get a breeze because the electric window was broke. Sheri thought she might try walking herself back into the JC's for her next shift because none of these dunces could hold two thoughts in their heads at once, and they'll have been drunk three times by then, so her transgression will have been replaced by some other drunken hook-up or trashiness du jour. What she hadn't expected though, hand to fucking god, was Son turning into a goddamned Corleone. She knew he had some weed priors, but leave it to Fortunato to spin her wheel, and now Sonny Corleone was drug-king-pinning with the Cuban cartel. Of course, Sheri would pick the stupid brother. Lessons learned, and this is why Sheri could depend only on Sheri and not goddamned Fortunato. She'd broken her own rule about interacting with anyone who might keep her from leaving this goddamned mill town.

As soon as Pigeon Forge Tony Montana left her alone to pick up Slim Jims and Mountain Dew. Could she listen to his ass do one more fucking impression of Randy Savage or called her Miss Elizabeth one more fucking time? She called the FBI tip line.

While it was ringing, Sheri realized she would need to do more than just narc on a tip line because she was tied way up in this mess as an accomplice to a drug transaction. She pulled up her big girl panties, hung up the phone, and placed a call to the Narcotics Unit of the Miami Police Department where she spoke to Sergeant Tony Hernandez. Sergeant Hernandez calmed her down, suggested they meet—certainly to size her and her story up—and she agreed. She told Sonny she needed to pick up some tampons and Marlboro Lights at the Quickpak and met Sergeant Hernandez. She agreed she would call him with the location of the meet and greet with the Cubans and the only thing she asked was that he let her go back to that sorry ass waitress gig at JC's.

Sheri called the Sergeant as soon as Son told her the plans. He was meeting the cartel at a bungalow off A1A in Little Havana. Sonny parked in an alley behind the bungalow, and told her to stay in the Blazer, like he had to tell her that shit.

She was planning to act as duct taped as the fucking seat cover. So, Sheri sees the police cars pull up silently after Sonny, suitcase in hand, clears the front door. She watches the lawmen cover the front and back of the house, knock, then storm inside. What she couldn't believe was Son rolling out of the window, suitcase in hand. This has been one fucking thing after another. So, there rolls Sonny out the window, and one of the officers who had been holding at the back door sees the movement and sprints across the backyard. He throws his arm up to tackle Son, clotheslining him. Sonny and the officer roll around for a minute until the policeman finally gets Sonny still. Honestly, she was home-free, and she didn't know what came over her at that moment, She didn't know if it was Sonny being so protective at JC's, her embarrassment at narcing Sonny out—how would she show her fucking face at home if they knew she'd called the cops—or if it was the weed she had smoked—she thought she'd just step outside the Blazer and holler, maybe wave the gun around to catch the cop's attention, so Sonny could get to the Blazer. So, she did just fucking that. She gets the cop's attention because she's flipping a shotgun around like a crazy person, but, and this is what she cannot forgive herself for, she didn't realize Sonny had slipped his Berreta Tom into his boot before they left the motel. Sonny pulls the Tom out and shoots the cop. What the fuck.

Sonny, feeling invincible with all the adrenaline and coke, hands her the suitcase and blows her a kiss because he now thinks they are dumbass Bonnie and Clyde. She jumps in that Blazer and pulls her ass around to the front yard of the bungalow because there is no way she's going to prison for any of this shit. She narced for god's sake.

Later, when she finally got back to the motel after hours at the police station does she finally realize that the dumbass had taken the wrong fucking suitcase to the meet and greet. Hell, he failed the fucking ASVAB.

Donna Wojnar Dzurilla

"Christabel"

Roland woke at the wheel of his '62 Chevy Impala to the shudder of the rear axle bottoming out in the center of the median strip that divided State Route 80 just outside of Clarion, Pennsylvania. The car swerved, out of his control, up the slope of the median to the westbound lanes. He'd been traveling east. The hollow sound of clumps of grass and dirt echoed off the wheel wells and bumper. He felt the clods of earth sucked up onto the car's underbelly. Chimes of gravel hit the bumper (or–fuck–maybe the custom paint job) in a distinctive four-four rhythm. His headlights bounced in time with the beat, and for a short time all he saw was hillside, grass, and weeds. Above, nothing but a moonless sky.

Roland spent months of work and lost track of the money he poured into restoring the twenty-two-year-old muscle car and obsessed over possible damage any time he hit the slightest bump in the road. Now this. Falling asleep at the wheel in the middle of the night in the middle of nowhere and lucky to land in the median strip. He deadheaded from Austin, Texas, straight through the last two days hoping to get back to State College before classes began after winter break if for no other reason than to enjoy an empty, quiet campus. Fucking students ruined a perfectly bucolic town.

He reached the crest of the median where it met the highway and stopped to regain his sense of direction. He knew how fast an unsuspecting truck driver hauling milk or gas or whatever-the-hell truckers transported on this godforsaken stretch of road traveled. He pulled slowly across the two westbound lanes before stopping on the shoulder. He kept his headlights on, tried and found the hazard light was dead. He tapped on the brake pedal and looked out the driver's side rear-view mirror, but no light appeared behind the car. Might just be a fuse and not a couple of burnt out bulbs. Bulbs for the Impala were a bitch to find, a bitch to change, and involved removing most of the taillight housing. Fuses, easy-peasy. Fuse box could be found attached to the fire wall behind the Impala's 400 V8 engine. He kept spare fuses in the trunk and the next time he stopped, he'd replace them. Couldn't risk catching a cop's attention.

Trees scarred white by acid rain and barren for winter lined both sides of the highway, occasionally sharing space with evergreens. A bit further down the road, the tree line broke and Roland made out what appeared to be a barn. No, Roland thought as he drew closer, a house. A faint light glowed in what looked to be an upper story window. That'd be somewhere he could pull over. He crept the car along the shoulder towards the light.

A big oak tree marked a break from the shoulder of the highway. Roland drew nearer, and just beyond the tree a green aluminum street sign illuminated by the Impala's headlights, read: Coal Ridge Road. He made a right off the gravel shoulder onto the asphalt and let the car coast down and stop in front of what appeared to be an abandoned mansion. He guessed it to have been built around the turn of the twentieth century, given its size and the state it was in.

A large bay window, all three windowpanes covered by plywood aged a flat black and split by the weather, offset a grand entrance of leaded beveled glass panels around an ornately carved set of oak doors. A porch ran along the front of the house and met the base of a rounded brick tower that rose up two stories. Steps to the porch had long since rotted away into chaotic rows on the ground. The steeply pitched roof angled to meet at the cross gables while decorative spindle work hung in varying degrees of disarray and deterioration from the gutters. From behind a single stained glass window panel on the grand house's second floor, the light that Roland saw from the highway flickered, as if from a candle. A red orchid, encircled in lead by a yellow snake, threw a soft orange light out onto what must have once been a formal garden.

A concrete fountain, with a trio of cherubs precariously balancing on the top tier, sunk to one side into the earth. The rusted wrought iron fence surrounding it stood upright, but settled to match the divets and rises of the plot of land.

The edge of the front seat's console stabbed his ribs as Roland leaned across the passenger seat to peer up at the window. He wondered what kind of family could afford to live in such a place and why they built it there. He instinctively pulled back when a shadow passed and darkened the illuminated orchid and snake. Someone watched him.

He wasn't looking for trouble. He had a delivery to make before he could crash at his apartment. Roland made a U-turn away from the mansion and drifted to a stop just before the road met the highway. He fished the flashlight out from under the driver's seat, put his foot on the brakes, and looked back one last time to confirm the taillights were out. After popping the latches for the trunk and hood he stepped out to the back of the car. The aroma of weed hit him and it took a few minutes to shuffle through the bricks and his luggage to find the box of fuses. It took less time to replace the fuses for the hazard and taillights than it did to fish them out of the trunk. He let gravity pull the hood down and pushed on it to lock it in place.

The wind picked up and rustled the leaves collected about the roots of the old oak. He felt eyes on him—and not just one set. Roland gazed over at the window, but the shadow had disappeared. A shiver passed through him that he attributed to the near freezing temperature and wind. He should have grabbed his winter coat from the back seat. He slid back into the driver's side of the Impala, but not before he heard a whistle, a long, slow cat call.

"That's some car you got there, mister," said a voice from beyond the oak. The moon finally moved from behind the clouds. Silver-white light reflected brightly off the crease of shiny tar where Coal Ridge met Route 80. It looked wet.

A young woman, no older than sixteen, looked in at him

through the driver's side window. Her pale skin took in the white-silver light of the moon and threw it right back out. She pulled a faded blue ribbon out to release her ponytail and let gravity and the wind take it. Roland couldn't take his eyes off of her and yet, out of the corner of his eye, felt compelled to watch the ribbon sink into the stream of moonlight that divided the road from highway. Her eyes were dark and matched the shadows behind her.

She reminded him of a girl he knew in high school. The girl, a year ahead of him, became the standard by which he evaluated all other women. He'd gotten the nerve to ask the girl out when he came upon her, alone at her locker one afternoon after lunch. She made him repeat himself because the first time he said it, she barely listened. The second time the girl told him to talk slower because she barely understood him. Nerves got to him. While Roland agreed with the idea that first loves were the truest loves, he'd never really had a first love—only a girl who didn't listen.

The girl rapped on the window to regain his attention. She stood a few feet from his door with a hand on her hip and pointed down the highway with her thumb. "Where you headed, mister?"

There was a pull in the air that made him want her. She lacked a coat, yet didn't appear cold. Her jeans were clean, but the terrycloth hooded sweatshirt she wore sagged in the front, as if it had been worn by another, chestier, woman. The sloppiness held sex. He was sure if he was close enough, he'd smell it on her. *Damn,* he thought *if I had someone who looked like her, she'd never leave the house.* He felt bewitched, but it might have just been the moonlight.

Nothing would amount to anything. He'd be an old man in her eyes.

"Onto State College. You live here?" he asked.

"Not anymore," she replied. A shadow crossed her face as the moon retreated back behind the clouds. "You a professor or something?" she asked.

"Something like that," Roland answered. "I work at the university."

"I'll ride along with you—that okay?"

Before Roland could answer, she dropped backside first into the passenger seat, then lifted her feet and swung her legs in. She avoided touching the metal doorframe. Once in, she said, "Christabel," as a way of introduction, then nodded, "and you are?"

"What are you doing out her at night, alone?" he asked. He tried his best to compose himself after watching how quickly and smoothly she moved into the bucket seat.

"I'm kind of lost, actually. I was partying in the woods back the road a piece and some guys started hassling me. I took off running and lost my way in the dark. I was happy to see your headlights."

Awful quick to have all that happen during the time he spent in front of the house, but he wasn't going to give her any shit about it. She didn't sound drunk or high, but hard to tell in the low light. Young girl out on the road alone wasn't safe.

"You can call me Christa if you like. Most do."

"Call me Roland. My name. Christabel is an old-fashioned name."

She smiled then reached and started fussing with the radio dial. She found a station, then turned the volume up.

"I thought you said you were headed to State College," she said. "You're going in the wrong direction."

"I know. I need to find somewhere to turn around or find an exit," Roland answered. "I don't remember seeing any exits, but I wasn't looking for them either."

The girl next to him turned in her seat and looked back at the house as he rolled onto the highway.

Christabel stood behind the stained-glass orchid and snake and watched Roland drive off with Geraldine. When she looked deep into the glass, it was Geraldine's face looking back. The white samite gown she wore belonged to Geraldine. She must have pulled it on by mistake in the middle of the night. After they'd finished. She'd been so, so cold. Christabel felt as if she'd never be warm again. She looked down at herself. The body beneath the gown filled it with curves bigger than her own.

Lyrics from a song by Cream wafted back towards Christabel as the Impala, taillights glowing, disappeared into the night.

I'll wait in this place where the sun never shines.
Wait in the place where the shadows run from themselves.

Patrick Michael Finn

"Broken End of Love"

She'd been teaching me how to get high and screw in her truck behind the Norco rodeo grounds, empty and anonymous in the offseason at the base of Mesquite Mountain and the Cactus Vista Hills. Her husband was overseas in the Marine corps.

We'd been meeting once or twice a week for the last six months when one night she pinched the flame dark and called everything off.

"My husband's coming home next week," she said.

The news made me pretty sad because the only other person in my life was my unemployed alcoholic father who was still mourning my mother, the woman who'd walked out on both of us three weeks after I was born.

By now I'd wanted to move out myself, but I was only sixteen and didn't yet have a job. I'd been cutting classes to look for one. Warehouses in Fontana and Colton, fast food, but nobody wanted me. I was starting to wonder if loneliness was contagious, and if shift managers and floor foremen could smell it on me.

"Next week," she said. "So we have to quit this. All of this."

"Man," I said.

"Man? Am I one of your little skateboard buddies?"

"I don't have any buddies," I said. "I don't even have a skateboard."

Maybe that's why I didn't feel too bad about carrying on with another man's wife. The way I looked at it, she was the one doing the cheating, while I was just along for this hot, secret ride.

"Oh, itty-bitty boy," she said. She touched my face. I hadn't noticed that she'd started crying. I felt a momentary rush of personal importance that flew off into the night hills behind us as soon as I remembered she was telling me goodbye.

The moon shone through the empty bleachers and pushed shadows of slats through the windshield.

She wiped a tear away and said, "And all along I was hoping you'd get me pregnant. We could have made a gorgeous baby."

"But I don't even have a job."

"Roland will think it's his," she said. "He won't know the difference. But I love him. He's been serving our country, and I can't be running around buying rubbers and Strawberry Spice perfume from Walgreens. You don't even notice that I'm wearing it."

"I do," I said. "It's real nice."

"Hell," she said.

"This is all nice," I said. "I'm going to miss your Strawberry Spice."

"What would you have named her?"

"Who?"

"The baby we could have made," she said.

"But we couldn't have. We were using condoms."

"If one of them broke then."

"William," I said.

"It would have been a girl, I know it," she said. "Besides, William's your name."

"Miss William, Junior," I said, and she lifted one side of her lips into the saddest half-smile I'd ever beheld.

I knew then that I'd just been shoved into the big condemned house of solitude. What I didn't know was how long I would live there, and how deeply that endless stretch of isolation would reach me. I was falling and falling off the broken end of love, or what love added up to at sixteen. I ended up landing in a black absence that never did find any further occupation.

Her last kiss barely grazed my cheek. She asked where she could drop me off. I told her I'd walk, and then I told her goodbye.

The Cactus Vista Hills were black against the moonlight. It was late October and cool at that hour. I wondered what shape my father would be in when I got home, and how much I'd have to clean up.

I followed the road under Interstate 15. A truck rushed overhead and crushed me to think it was hers. It sounded like a wave rolling onto the shore. It was the only sound in the whole world, and I was the only one left to hear it.

Scott Gould

The Five Pound Bass—Every Sunday

If you were to ask me, I wouldn't know what to call it. It could be irony. Or fate. Fate always pokes its head up the way fate will do. Some people might call it funny, the way it all went down that morning. I can see the hint of humor there. These days, it's just more sad than anything else. And if I were to think hard about it, I'm not sure there was any way to prevent it. The world is going to spin no matter which way we tilt.

And you can't put all the blame on the fishing. Fishing was a symptom of some larger illness, which I have come to believe is always the case. Men don't fish for the sheer joy of catching a pea-brained creature on a piece of sharp jewelry. They fish because they are supposed to be doing something else. Somebody's always trying to catch the fisherman.

All those sounds every Sunday morning—the crinkle of the plastic when he pulled his honey bun from the microwave and unwrapped it and whispered, *Shit that's hot*. The jangle when he grabbed the key to the gate off its hook. He told me once he was the only civilian Odom gave a key to. The clink of the deadbolt sliding, and finally, the drumroll of his pickup pulling away. Then, the silence, silence I liked for a few weeks after we started sleeping together under one roof. Time to do whatever I wanted. But when those weeks eddied into a year, I began to hate every Sunday.

Once, I told him, "Rikard, we should go to church. You can fish some other morning." He stared at me like men do. You know, that look that suggests they truly believe they have knowledge. "Read your Bible, sweet cheeks," he said. "Jesus loves him a man who fishes." You cannot argue with someone when they start propping Jesus up as evidence.

He told me—more than one time—about his Sunday morning routines, thinking I was interested. How he would stop by the Grab N Go and top off his tank and buy a Stewart sandwich from the cooler in the back. That was his lunch. That time of morning, Rikard said, when the sun was just feathering the clouds in the east, in the direction of Olanta and New Zion, the game warden would be standing faithfully at the counter of the Grab N Go, filling up on coffee and Krispy Kremes.

According to Rikard, the warden always checked his license, but wasn't a jerk about it. Always did it with a smile on his face, a smile bordered with sugary donut glaze.

"Where you heading, Rikard?" Lester would ask.

"You know where," Rikard would answer, grinning.

"I might have to run out there, check on you. Check your limit," Lester would say.

"Only keep what I can eat and that ain't never enough," Rikard would say.

"How'd you get Odom to let you fish his pond? What you got on him? You know where the bodies are buried or something?"

"My personality opens doors that otherwise remain closed," Rikard would say and hand his fishing license over for inspection. One time, Rikard told me, Lester left a greasy, glazed thumbprint on the corner that never went away. Rikard was proud of that smudge for some reason.

Every Sunday, I lay there, imaging what Rikard was doing. Him backing the pickup through the waist-high dog fennel, sliding his jon boat out of the bed. Shoving off from the bank, one foot in the boat, one in the mud at the water's edge. Him, looking around for water moccasins swimming toward the fresh ripples, thinking their breakfast had come for a dip. Rikard, paddling with one hand, reaching for his rod with the other. Him, scanning the bank for cover that might be holding bass. Rikard never cared about bream or redbreast. He only wanted bass. I know all this because I know Rikard. You know somebody well enough, your mind's eye can go on cruise control. You see it all without trying.

Maybe that's part of it. Rikard still performed all his normal routines because we lived in his house. He didn't have to give anything up just because I took over three drawers and half a closet. He still made all those Sunday morning noises, still sat at the kitchen table a couple of nights a week, fiddling with his tackle box. He would spread his lures across the Formica, dividing them into categories only he could name. I saw a rainbow pile of worms, the funk of rotten plastic filling the air above the table. Lures that looked like miniature fish, trailing hooks below them. Rikard called them treble hooks, which made me think of music and not water. He sharpened his hooks with a tiny file. "When I latch onto something," he'd say, "I don't like letting it get away."

What bored me most were the knots. He made me sit…okay, that's harsh. He didn't make me. He asked me to sit, and I did, because I wanted him happy, and maybe I wanted to camouflage myself a bit, hide behind some fake interest in his pieces of twine.

"Now, this here," he'd say, "is the knot most folks use." He'd snort. "And they wonder why they lose fish." He wound one end of the twine around the other, then doubled back on itself through a loop. "Clinch knot."

He untangled it. "But here, this is better. This is why I don't lose bass when I set the hook." To me, it looked like the same exact thing, except for one little doo-dad at the end that seemed more for show than anything else. "That there is your improved clinch knot. Everything wraps around itself an extra time, sort of. Stays put." He tugged hard on the two free ends and the knot snapped tight. And every time those ends pulled taut, I'd smile at him. Probably a mistake, I know, giving a man the wrong idea about his hooks and knots.

But I had my limits. For instance, I couldn't be around while he gutted the bass outside at the spigot, then brought the emptied-out carcass into the kitchen. Once, he tried to show me how to slide that thin, sharp filet knife down the backbone and over the ribs. "These are the best size to filet," he said. "Around five pounds." I couldn't watch, but I ate the hell out of the filets he had me fry up in the cast iron skillet he kept under the sink, wrapped in greasy paper towels. That probably says something about me. The fact I couldn't watch the hard part—the gutting and cutting—but I didn't mind enjoying the aftereffects. Makes me wonder about the kind of person I am.

Which is all to say, the wondering and confusion and fake smiling all came to a head one Sunday morning. Rikard went through his routines—the yawn-and-stretch at the dark edge of the bed, the hack to clear the night from his throat, the plastic honey bun, the beeps of the microwave, the deadbolt sliding open and racking back, the ignition in the driveway. The silence.

I didn't have to turn the lights on to find my way to the front door. I'd come to know the topography of Rikard's house with my eyes closed. I flowed around the furniture in the blackness and found the deadbolt like I was reading Braille. Slid it open. I had a brand-new routine of my own.

A half hour later, Lester parked his pickup a quarter mile away on a side road and slipped across the side yard and through the front door, then inside. New sounds had begun filling my gray Sunday light—Lester looping his gun belt over the chair. Him, flipping the little notebook he carried onto the dresser. I told him once to be careful and not spread too much of himself around; he might forget something one Sunday. He said, "I don't forget things like that," and I have to say, he never failed to pick up his belongings on the way out.

Don't think bad of me. Rikard and I weren't married. I wasn't wrecking a family. I was not aiming a torpedo at a pile of marriage vows. I was just tired of being part of somebody's routine. That's human nature, right? I didn't plan on it. I had no plot in mind for this particular story. You know how these things start, with the tiniest of motions. The two of you in the same aisle in the produce section. Or a wave across the gas pumps. Suddenly, I started seeing Lester's government-green truck everywhere, that big whip antennae like a signal flag for some fresh twitch in my gut. I figured I'd earned it, what with having to watch all those hooks being sharpened and all those knots being tied.

That one Sunday, the last one, me lying there with Lester, the two of us watching the new light of morning seep around the blinds. Him telling me about his day. More routines. "I got to run out to the landing in Kingstree and check licenses and boat registrations. Then I got to drive to Andrews and make sure those Lewis boys ain't baiting their dove fields again. You know, same old, same old."

And he was right. *Same old, same old.* Men and their routines. It must make them comfortable to do the same things over and over. Lester rolled onto me, which was probably why we didn't hear the truck roll up in the pea gravel. Rikard was in a hurry—I could tell by the footsteps across the hardwoods in the living room. Before I could make a move, I heard Rikard snatch the key to Odom's gate from its hook.

Dammit, that's right, I thought, *I didn't hear that sound this morning. He broke his routine.*

Lester froze where he was for a second, then rolled quietly to Rikard's side of the bed and pulled the covers to his chin. Not hiding exactly, more like a little kid waiting for the clap of thunder after lightning strikes in the yard.

Rikard stuck his head in the bedroom door and was halfway through announcing that he'd forgotten the key when he saw the shape of Lester beside me in the half-light. For a couple of seconds, they just stared at each other, their eyes not blinking, reminding me of those bass that get filleted, their eyes wide but not really seeing.

Rikard said, "You naked under there, Lester?" as if that would make a difference. Before Lester could answer, Rikard glanced to the right and saw the gun belt and the thick, camo pants on the chair. "Never mind," Rikard said. I tensed up, watching to see if Rikard would go for the gun. I was betting against it.

I expected man sounds, big noises. Shouts or excuses or explanations. I don't understand men.

"Where's your truck?" was all Rikard said.

"That gravel turnaround in Alvin's soybean field," Lester said.

"I don't suppose you got a license for this sort of thing," Rikard said, and I saw a smile creeping its way toward the corners of his mouth.

"I ain't even sure it's in season," Lester said, and quickly, suddenly, they were fine with each other, and I was alone, under that thick quilt, outnumbered by the fishermen on a Sunday morning. Nobody wanted to fight over me, fight me until I tired out at the end of their line. Lester rustled under the covers.

"I don't suppose you'll be here when I get back," Rikard says, then points at me. "I'm talking to you."

Something about setting the hook ran through my head. Something about catch and release. I wanted to ask Lester what kind of knot we were dealing with. Was this a clinch knot or was it an improvement? It didn't feel like this was going to be all that hard to untie. Things get away.

But you know how fishing stories are. The more they get told, the bigger it all gets. I wonder what Rikard and Lester talk about at the Grab N Go now, on those mornings before the sun is up good. I wonder if they make up more and more details every Sunday. I wonder if Rikard still gets his license checked. I imagine the glaze on those doughnuts. That's what I think about some Sundays—not every Sunday, just here and there—as I lie alone in the dark and in the silence and imagine what sounds are missing.

Bobby Horecka

"Corpus Christi Bay—Just One of the Band"

So, how about a Guy Clark song, maybe, or… something Delbert McClinton wrote, perhaps? Ya know, something that resonates… a good song… That last part just hung out there for a moment, like Christmas lights on a shithouse. Did he have the foggiest notion who he was talking to? Truth be told, he did have him one nice head of hair, far as fellas went. All curly like but neat, ya know? And he was just doing his job, best way he knew how. Ain't easy keeping a buncha n'er-thee-wells like us all headed the same direction long, yet he'd managed to do so for right at six hours already. O'course, like usually happens with this sorta thing, you can't very well un-say something, once it's out there, floating about the universe.

Still, calling the ol' boy Scrote, probably did cross a line somewhere, even if he did seem to take a real shine to it. We were just having us a little fun is all. Joke him if he can't take a fuck, right?

You should've seen him, though, just lit right up whenever ol' Bill said it.

Ol' Scrote knows, he'd say. Ain't that right, Scrote?

He'd get this big dumbass grin on his face, them eyes a his just shining big and bright. Like I got no idea what the fuck you fellas are talking about, but I'm gonna stand here and grin, just the same. Show you all my teeth, all at once.

I bet the ol' boy felt like he was really one of us now, you know? One of the band. Got him an authentic road name and everything, by God. He was ready for the big time now, ready to saunter on up and just—ah, who am I kiddin'? Just fuckin' nothin' is what he'd do. He couldn't play a fuckin' radio if he tried. That much was obvious. And considering he'd proven to be right near goddam tone deaf the whole day thus far, this sumbitch wouldn't last ten minutes out on the road. Still the boss heard he was some kinda child genius when it came to putting an album together, so we spent the better part of a day amusin' and painful, all at the same time. He'd just stand there, scratching away, just a-grinnin' his ass off at all of us, who were just a grinnin' right back at him. O'course, we were all stoned. Grinnin' came natural to us. He was doing it sober as Sunday school, though.

Hey, you wanna hit? Joey, our road man, had asked him, not long after we all got there. In asking, he offered up this monster roll of some truly primo Kush that Joey's wife grew special for us out on the Reservation. We'd been burning that thing half the day already, seemed like, and we were still only about half done. Thing was fat around as a Cuban Montescristo and just smooth as glass.

You would've thought ol' Joey was handing him a whole pile of live rattlesnakes, the way he skedaddled his way back to that sound booth. Nearly broke his ass trying to get away. Like the shit was gonna reach out and bitch slap him to the ground, and take his lunch money before it turned him into some longhaired freak like one of us. He was backin' up, waggin' his arms back and forth like he was swatting bees or something. Then he started stammerin' something about how he done gave it up on account of his business or some damn thing, a point he drove home by holding his hands out front of him and pushing like hell. Looked like he was either about to pinch a loaf right there on the carpet in front of God and nation, or he was trying to make like one of them damn mimes, trying to stop a car with his bare hands or get out of some kinda damn box that only he could see.

But if you fellas wanna have your fun, he hollered over his shoulder, I-I-I sure ain't gonna stand in your way. That's how he said it, too: I-I-I... And he was off, scamperin' off to his sound booth, faster than a nine-year-old who just got popped looking through the peep hole into the girls locker room, all so he could put some solid walls twixt us and him. Like I say, he was wound pretty tight for the kind of work we do. Just a matter a time before one of the guys started fuckin' with him, and Bill just happened to be that guy.

Why the boss seemed so all-fired impressed with the kid, I'll never comprehend. Seemed like more of a knob to us, and given the last six hours, I believe ol' Robert Earl was starting to come around to our way of thinking, no matter what it was he'd heard about the little shitass.

Still, he was almost too easy to fuck with. Absolutely no challenge whatsoever. That he probably had a little Rain Man thing happening was obvious, but more than that, it broke your heart a little just seeing his face go all glowy whenever ol' Bill hollered it out, if you're the type that gets all weepy over such shit. We been on the road so damn long with Robert Earl, nothing fazed us much anymore. Most of us didn't even have an address anymore other than wherever that bus was parked. That ol' tour bus of his was our home. It was kinda like Willy's Honeysuckle Rose, only ours probably smelled a lot more like it did back when him and Waylon used to tour together—unwashed feet, dried sweat, skid-marked drawers you had on for two days longer than you should have, and chain-smoked Marlboro Menthols to try and cover up the weed somebody was always passing around. Last time I climbed aboard Willy's rig, the damn thing smelled like vanilla wafers, something his ol' lady saw to these days, which is why we don't allow women on our bus no more. To start, ain't none of us what anybody might mistake for youngsters no more. We hadn't had that problem in years now, so the thought of getting a little side action on the road just didn't hold the allure it once did. And sure, having a woman around would probably make it a lot easier to breathe in there, but next thing you know, they'd have you doing crazy shit, like eating kale granola or taking bubble baths or some shit. Remember the last time ol' Willy got pinched on some dope? What the papers didn't tell you was Robert Earl and crew was stepping off his bus about the same time the law come busting in. Can't believe those cocksuckers actually hauled him in for that. Hell, he's an old man with glaucoma. Let him be, for Chrissake. Besides, it's hardly some state secret that Willy's probably got some primo stash out somewhere in his immediate vicinity. If he ain't on stage, he's likely partaking. Took some real stellar detective work to sniff that out, let me tell you.

You know his momma had to be damn proud.

Willy had a lot more class about the whole thing than I probably would have. They sent me in to go bail him out and fetch him back to the bus, but this jackass reporter caught us, soon as we stepped outside. He's just hammering away with questions that there really ain't a good answer to. So, what's it like getting popped for dope at your age. Again. I mean, what is this, the 2,000th time now? Willy just kinda shrugged like he didn't savvy no English right then. Would've thought our hombre there might've taken a hint, but no. He just tried a different tact.

Just how much did they pop you with? he asked.

I dunno, Willy answered. About a dime bag, I guess. We already smoked up the rest.

Already smoked up the rest, eh? Our reporter suddenly went all Baptist church deacon on us, shaking his head in disapproval, judging Willy fuckin Nelson, if you can believe that shit.

What kinda example do you think that sets for our young people? he asked him. About a dime bag... You should be ashamed of yourself.

As we boarded the bus, Willy stopped on the steps, turned to him and said one of funniest fuckin' things I'd ever heard up to then.

At least it wasn't a bag of spinach, he told him…

You know, 'cause people was straight shittin' themselves to death at the time, all traced back to some bad spinach that found its way to the store shelves. It was all over the radio… So, it was like all he had was just a dime bag of weed, not that deadly spinach shit, right?

Guess you had to be there, to truly appreciate it.

It was funny as fuck, though, we all thought.

And that's why we never let women on the bus. They'd have

you shitting yourself into the grave after cramming big wads of spinach down your gullet, claiming it was good for your health. Until you start shittin' yourself to death, I suppose. Besides, that damn bus of ours smelled bad enough as it was without all that happy horse shit to boot, I tell you…

Ain't that right Scrote?

Ol' Bill was at it again.

And there goes Scrote, just the biggest grinning dumbass you ever did see.

Let's do Corpus Christi Bay, Robert Earl says then. And a one, and a two and a…

That's where I came in. I play the guitar, you see. And a little fiddle every now and then. Ol' Bill, he's the bass man and Tommy there, he's our drummer and designated joint roller. He's taken it to its own artform. The joints, I mean. Because there's a hellova lot better drummers out there. Ain't too many can match his joint rolling, though. We met up with ol' Robert Earl on Sixth Street back in 1978 and basically been with him ever since.

Ol' Scrote finally seemed to find something he could "groove to," as he put it, and that was a damn ugly sight: him, grooving. Looked like he ran the zipper up over his foreskin and was presently psyching himself up to rip that fucker back down, but he kept wussin' out at the last possible second. That's what this cat's "grooving" looked like. Hate to see what he'd look like if that zipper mishap ever really did happen.

It was fuckin strange enough that even ol' Bill got concerned about the little dipshit. You doing alright up there, Scrote? he asked over the mic as we wrapped up our song.

The kid's instantly a grinning dumbass once more.

That shore was fine right there, the kid said.

He sounded like a cross between Pappy O'Daniel and Foghorn Leghorn. Didn't help none that he was still spazzing out up there like he was having a goddam seizure.

Shore was fine, he said again. That's what I'm talking about, right there…

If I didn't know any better I'd swear it was the first time he ever heard the fuckin' song. Surely Robert Earl wasn't asking some punk kid how to arrange our next album when he wasn't even familiar with our work. What kinda rock had he been living under? Only been three decades since we released it. Pretty much everybody is bound to have heard that tune at least once by now.

Just then, Robert Earl leaned in real close.

I'm gonna go talk with this kid and see what he's got going on, he said. Y'all don't stray too far. We got places to be.

And off he went, headed for the sound booth. As he did, ol' goofy came back on the comms and caught us all off guard.

So, what's that mean, anyhow? the boy asked. A Scrote. Is that some kinda drum thing? I can't say I'm familiar with it.

Oh shit. Even Robert Earl stopped dead in his tracks on that one, as we all spun around to see how Ol' Bill might dig his ass out of this bullshit. I was nervous, just sitting between the two of them, but ol' Bill had no fucks left to give whatsoever. He didn't even try to sugarcoat the sumbitch any…

A Scrote is, you know, like a scrotum, just a little shorter is all. A nut sack if you will. We been playing our asses off out here all damn day, and you keep drifting in and out, going back and forth between being an outright dick and a genuine asshole, so I figured you come by it honest. I mean, that's where them little wrinkled bastards tend to hang out, ain't it? Hell, you even got the curly hair. I figured you must be some kinda kindred.

He did have the curls, that's the God's honest truth. He couldn't argue that none…

Ol' Bill having clearly made all the points he intended for the moment, we all spun back around to see how Scrote was taking it all. I gotta say, it was probably better than a lot of folks might've who'd just got dick-slapped by a big ol' bowl of honesty like that. At least that big dumbass grin was gone. Made him look a lot less like a retard, which was a good thing for a fella like him. He definitely had some kinda Rain Man thing happening there, the more I thought about it. Yeah, definitely, yeah.

Bet he was a damn fine driver, too…

Plus, he'd quit that awful gyrating he'd been doing, too, which was another step in the right direction for the ol' boy. That's about where all the positives seemed to taper off, though. From there, it just got uncannily quiet for a sound studio. That's when we noticed the ol' boy started turning red. Thought he was blushing at first, embarrassed, you know. I mean, who wouldn't be? He just had a guy calling him a nut sack all morning and he mistook it all for a term of endearment. I'd be feeling not quite myself, too, if I was him.

But then that red started going full-on purple. Looked like he had a wad of bacon stuck in his craw or some such. We were just about to go Heimlich his ass when he finally spoke up. By then, he had a noticeable twitch going on and that stammering of his was back with a vengeance.

I-I-I th- think y'all need t-t-to go, he managed to get out, never once looking up at us. He just kept his face down and eyes fixed way off in the distance, you know, not really focused on any one thing. Robert Earl sure wasn't waiting for it in writing. He scooted on back to where he'd been and started grabbing his stuff.

Pack your shit, boys. Let's get the hell outa here, he said.

I picked up my guitar case and started flicking open the latches. Tommy was busy trying to scoop up the weed he'd dumped out on his snare drum almost as soon as that last song ended, intending to roll one. Now he was trying not to spill it all so he could take the damn thing apart. About the only fellas not moving was Ol' Scrote up in the booth, who looked like he might have an aneurism at any moment, and ol' Bill, who was standing there, all strapped up still like he's gonna play another set right quick before he scooted out the door.

What? Bill said, eyeballing us like a bunch of traitors. You was all thinking it. I just had the balls to say it out loud.

He probably could've done without the mention of balls yet again because ol' Scrote seemed to take it pretty hard. He went from being kinda miffed but calm to sounding precisely like what I imagine the wrath of God might be like, especially when he piped in over them damn loudspeakers:

GET... THE FUCK... OUT... OF MY STUDIO! He said, his voice ringing in every instrument we had, before he said it again, and then again, the odd pauses necessary because he needed more air to continue on. He seemed to expend every last ounce he had just saying the words. The effect was booming and recoiling off every surface in there. It began to take on the sound of rolling thunder. It was about the most impressive thing we'd seen him do, the entire time we'd been there.

What's eating him? Bill said, just before Scrote fired off again, only louder this time, meaner, more roar-like.

That finally motivated Bill to action. He' finally unstrapped and was reaching for his case, too. Tommy's already got the toms and snare broke down and is headed out to the bus, one under each arm. Robert Earl is right behind him, a guitar case in each hand. I'm not far behind, though Bill's already fallen into step behind Robert Earl. A couple trips later and we got the whole shebang. We're cruising down the highway before anybody dared speak again. It was Bill, wouldn't you know, like he ain't said plenty already.

That kinda reminded me of that shrimper, out on the bay that day we flipped the car, he said. What? Robert Earl said, annoyed and spinning around. You mean from the song?

Well yeah.

Well, sorry, we got drunk and flipped car into some random shrimp boat that was passing by out on the bay with one mad-as-hell shrimp boat captain aboard who was ready gut your ass for saying something asinine after sinking his boat in five foot of water just don't work near as well as a song lyric. Besides, nobody would've believed we pulled off that kinda Duke boy bullshit, even if we had found a way to fit it all in the song. Hell, I was there and still don't believe it. And we don't need to relive every fuckin' detail in the songs we sing either. That we ain't still making payments for that chickenshit boat is nothing short of a miracle, all by itself.

Bill accepted his reprimand with grace. Well, as much of that shit as he could muster, anyhow, and we traveled several miles in silence before he spoke up again.

I was always kinda touched you called me your brother in that song, Bill said then. The words sapped every bit of energy Robert Earl might've had left at the moment, no matter how much he still wanted to chew on ol' Bill's ass. He'd spun around like he was about to give Bill the what for, but that asinine comment was all he really said on the subject. He'd sat there steaming, like he had more to say for a while now, but he never did come up with the right words, I guess. He finally spun back around in his seat.

I know one of you boys is bound to have it rolled up by now, he said. Spark that shit up!

And we did, and he did, and we all did together. And nobody said shit for a good long while. We just let good herb do what it does best and take some of the edge off as we watched the world scoot on by out our windows. Finally, Robert Earl broke the silence. I was really counting on that kid to give us some direction, he said.

Aw, we don't need that little shit, Tommy piped in. You never steered us wrong before, Skipper.

His words hung there a while, like the cloud of pot smoke that hung thick in the air around us. It would take one hellova lot of menthols to cover that up, that much was certain. We made a few more miles before Robert Earl finally responded.

Well, there was that one time, down by the seawall when we hit that shrimp boat that was passing by on the bay.

We couldn't help ourselves. That was some funny shit, right there.

Now it was, at least. Not so much at the time. We were all just kids still when that happened. I was scared shitless back then.

After a good laugh, we all paused while we caught our breath, still not really sure if Robert Earl was gonna be OK. He paid that little prick quite a bit of money, only to get run off after Bill opened his big yap about nut sacks. Good chance the boss might need a day or two of wound lickin' still.

Or not...

Like a scrotum but shorter, where the little wrinkled bastards hang out, so to speak.

We figured you was kindred.

Robert Earl was laughin' so hard he shook.

We gotta put that shit to music somehow, he said. That's fucking hilarious...

It's no Road Goes on Forever, albeit, but it'll do in a pinch.

And just like that, we were golden once more. Like the song said, too, we never could stay sober, out by that damn bay. We smoked most of the rest of what we had as we wheeled on down the highway. It was the least we could do after all we'd seen together, and not nearly enough after all we'd been through.

I was glad to be headed for the Hill Country, though. It was just safer there for fellas like us.

Patti Meredith

"No Kinda Dancer—Phantom Partner"

Working at a dance hall was something I never thought I'd do. But when push comes to shove, you surprise yourself. I was living outside of Blanco with the kids. Their daddy was an oil rigger, gone for a month at a time. I should have known when he moved us from Corpus Christi where he worked offshore that something was up. Darrell said Corpus was getting too crowded.

He said he wanted to get back up to the hill country where he grew up, that he needed space around him. Moving away from all I knew didn't make much sense, but what did back then? I was nineteen with two little ones a year apart.

That Sunday, Darrell left like he always did. "See you in a few," he'd said. I cried and stood outside the trailer with the kids until his truck got out of sight. I hated to see him go, but I remember feeling lucky. I remember thinking we had a future. I remember being crazy about the way he'd spot me from far off and grin. When he didn't call that night like he said he would, I called him and didn't get an answer. I worried there'd been an accident on the rig, so I called a buddy of his in Corpus. He said, "No, ain't nothing happened."

But something had happened. I thought maybe Darrell's phone had quit working, so I called Maverick Oil, but since me and him weren't married, they wouldn't give me a number for the rig.

I called his mama even though she and I'd never took to one another, and she said, "I don't know nothing about it." That didn't sound right. What "it" was she talking about?

The end of the week I heard from a girlfriend that Darrell had moved in with a woman he met in Lake Charles. He wasn't even on the rig. Turns out, I'd been left. He'd dumped me and the kids on the side of a dirt road like a box of kittens nobody wanted.

I was set on going to Corpus. I wanted Darrell to tell me to my face that we were done, but I knew my old Toyota wouldn't make the trip. I called my brother, and he said, "I could come get you, but then what? There ain't nowhere for you down here." And that was the truth. Our mama was in Oklahoma with her boyfriend, and my sisters were all put out with me for one thing or another.

I had four hundred dollars in my checking account and the man we rented from said Darrell had paid up through July. It came to me that he'd planned ahead and wasn't coming back.

I wished I could get mad and hate him. Instead, I thought about the morning he left and tried to figure out what I'd done to make him leave.

Our trailer was down a dirt road off the highway. About a half mile from ours, two more sat side by side. Women were always sitting around down there in white plastic chairs smoking cigarettes underneath the live oaks. Darrell said they must be a bunch of whores, but they looked like regular folks to me.

One morning a girl was at her mailbox when I drove by. I slowed down and introduced myself. She said her name was Ashley and she lived in one trailer and her mama lived in the other. "You know of any jobs around here?" I ask her. "I got to get me some work."

"You dance?" she said. "You know the two-step? The polka?"

"Yeah, my granny taught me when I was a kid."

"Well, old man Harvey down at the dance hall's looking for a girl to wait tables and dance with the cowboys. The longer they hang around, the more they drink. I'm going tonight if you want to go. Mr. Harvey'll give you thirty dollars a night and you drink for free." She looked off down the road. "What you do out in the parking lot is up to you, and he don't want to hear about it."

"I got kids," I said. Nodding to Jimmy and Katie who were making a fuss in the backseat.

"Mama'll keep 'em. She likes kids."

A night out sounded good to me, thirty dollars or not, so I went that first night. The dance hall, a tinned-roofed, old gray building with tall white windows, sat back off the road. It wasn't even dark when we got there, and the parking lot was already filling up. Old folks, young folks, kids, men in boots and cowboy hats, all yelling "howdy" to one another like it was a big family reunion. Inside, white Christmas lights hung from rough rafters and a mirror ball flickered light across the shiny floor. Somebody had even wound lights around the wagon wheels hanging down from the ceiling. A band on a little stage played an oom-pah song I remembered from when Granny would take us kids to a dance hall down in Cat Springs.

Ashely introduced me to Mr. Harvey, and he put me to work. Right after I took my first tray of beers to a long, wooden table in the back, an old boy grabbed hold of me and swung me around 'til I thought I'd faint from the dizzy head.

At eleven o'clock, Mr. Harvey turned the bright lights on, his way of saying the night was over. He gave me and Ashley and two other girls our money and made sure we got to our cars without being bothered.

Funny now to think how innocent we were.

When August came around and my money was fixing to run out, me and the kids moved in with Ashley and she helped me get a shift at the Waffle House. I told myself when I got my car running, I'd go to Corpus, find Darrell, and straighten things out, but by the time I could afford to get one part replaced, another would break down.

One Saturday, the first cool night of the summer, a man came in the dance hall looking like he'd wandered in the wrong door. He was stocky and clean-cut with jet-black hair. He kept his hands in the pockets of his Khaki pants and took a seat at a back table.

"What can I do for you," I said.

"I'll have a Coca-Cola."

"You don't like beer?"

He smiled. "Teetotaler." He stuck out his hand and I took it. "Ralph Gunter."

"I'm Sara McKenzie," I said, not being used to introductions. When I brought him his Coke, he was looking out at the dance floor, "Who's that fellow?"

I knew he meant Woodrow, the old man who came in every now and again to dance with his ghost. The first time I saw him waltzing around, arms hanging in the air, eyes shut, it kind of spooked me. But the girls said he used to come with his wife, then after she died, he started coming back alone. I thought how I'd lie in bed and pretend Darrell still slept beside me. Me and Woodrow weren't that different.

"That's Woodrow," I said. "His wife died. He comes in and dances like that. I reckon it makes him feel like she's still around."

Ralph got a real sad look on his face.

"You like to dance?" I said, wanting to cheer him up.

He shook his head. "I'm no kind of dancer."

"You ever tried?"

"Not really," he said with a smile. "I come from Baptists."

"Y'all don't dance?" Thinking about that now, I bet he thought I was ignorant, and I was. I didn't know a thing about church folks.

"Come on," I said. "I'll show you."

He looked again at Woodrow. "I guess I could try."

I took his hand and Ralph Gunter and I danced until closing. We started with a waltz, then when the band played "Roll Out the Barrel" I tried to show him the polka steps, but he didn't catch on right away. We got to laughing and some of the other girls came out and helped.

The next Saturday, Ralph came in with bluebonnets wrapped in a piece of damp newspaper. He led me to the dance floor, and when the band struck up, I could tell he'd been practicing. Trouble was, Ralph kept me dancing all night.

Mr. Harvey didn't give me a dime. "I ain't paying you for courtin' a teetotaler."

Ralph had come to Blanco to manage his brother's plumbing supply store, and sometimes he could go on too long talking about water heaters, but he was good company. He'd lived with his mother in Houston until she died and was looking for a fresh start. He said he'd almost married once, but it didn't work out. I didn't push for details. I didn't want him asking me about mine. All I said was that the kids' daddy was out of the picture.

Ralph liked to take me to dinner at T.J.'s Steakhouse. He got the air conditioner working in the trailer and paid to get the Toyota running. He was good with Jimmy and Katie, and when September came, he took us all to the Texas State Fair in Dallas. Ashely said I'd hit the jackpot.

Ralph was a gentleman. The first I'd ever known. He didn't paw at me like the boys I was used to. His kisses were sweet, and we did okay in the sack. Nothing fancy, but nice. On our six-month anniversary, Ashley said, "I bet he's going to pop the question." She was sitting on my bed, and I was getting dressed. Since dating Ralph, I'd put on weight and nothing I liked fit anymore.

"What would you do?" I said.

"I'd marry him."

I gave her the side-eye. "Bull hockey."

Ashley had a type. Tall, lanky cowboys. Slow talkers with drowsy eyes. Men like Darrell.

That night, Ralph and I went to T.J.'s. and when our usual waitress brought us our pie, she had funny look on her face. I thought maybe she knew something I didn't. Later, at the dance hall, Ashley's mama came in with Jimmy and Katie. I didn't know they were coming but Ralph scooped up Katie and I danced with Jimmy to the "Tick Tock Polka." We were having the best time. I couldn't help but think if Ralph did ask me to marry him, I might say yes.

Then Jimmy let go of my hand and took off for the door. "Daddy!"

I've been back in Corpus now for a couple of years. Darrell and I didn't stay together long. The kids still talk about Ralph, about the time he took us to the fair. And I think of him, too. His strong shoulders. The smooth feel of those starched shirts. The weight of his hand on my waist when he waltzed me around.

I think about Woodrow, dancing with his ghost. Sometimes, in my mind, I get the two mixed up.

Memoir

Kimberly Parish Davis

"Willie"
for Daddy

Robert Earl Keen must have had a grandma with pictures of his grandpa or his dad riding a broodmare with a stud colt named Willie trailing along beside her, because he wrote a song about a photograph hanging faded on the wall. At least, my mind's eye sees it as faded. Our old photos like that have faded now to the point where it's hard to make out details.

There's one old picture I can't find anymore where Daddy balanced a baby me up on his stud horse's back. The horse's name was Hobo Adam, and he was the sire of Bo's Hope and grandsire of Bo Diamond Dandy and some other notable horses my mother loved through the rest of her life. Old Hobo Adam had a barn burn down on him, and his back was covered in scars, so he was never ridden by the time I came along. He was black with a white blaze face and white socks, and he passed those characteristics to his offspring. One of his daughters, Bo's Hope, was black with a completely white face the horse people call a bald face. She had blue eyes, and four white socks that went all the way to her knees—flashy. Mom always said she almost had too much white on her to be registered as a Quarter Horse. It would have been like the end of the world to have to register a horse as a Paint. Both my parents were snotty like that. And Mom got even snottier as she and my stepdad transitioned from being horse trainers to racehorse breeders.

I always knew Daddy was a scoundrel. He lived with another woman for most of the week selling property up around the Trinity River at the time my parents broke up. I know now that other things happened, and it wasn't completely one-sided, and I've forgiven Mom. Notice I call my mother Mom, not Mommy. Around the time she and Daddy divorced she became Mom to me. She was fragile, broken, and that somehow put us on an even footing, no longer each other's darlings, but combatants fighting against the world together. I understand her a lot better now, and I'm sad for her.

Daddy loved country music almost as much as he loved women and horses, but I don't think Mom or Daddy either one ever heard Keen's song, "Willie." Funny how I still want to call him Daddy, with a y on the end, like the diminutive "-ito" you can tack onto the ends of words in Spanish to indicate a thing is a small one or a baby one. In English, the -y at the end of Daddy sweetens Dad, elevates him to an adoring child's-eye view. But Daddy, scoundrel though he was, I still think of him with the y on the end.

But the photo in the song isn't so faded that the singer can't make out dandelions in the field, so it's spring or early summer, which makes the stud colt a few months old, since we always bred the registered mares so they would foal as early in the year as we could, because the horses' official birthdays were the first of the year. Therefore, foals born early in the year were naturally bigger than others they'd be competing with. I'm mixing up the time frames, though. The horse shows and racetracks came later, but I imagine Willie from the song as playful and strong… probably not sticking too close to his mama's side anymore. You can't be sure a colt like that won't bounce past, take a bite out of your leg just for fun, and run off into the road. They're like teenagers.

Keen's ol' cowboy is riding through a field. I guess there wouldn't be too many places for the colt to run off and get hurt there, but when I rode with Daddy, when I was little, we rode beside the road. I had an old palomino gelding called Rebel, and Daddy would hook a lead rope onto Rebel's halter to tow us along behind him. He whistled and sang to keep me and Rebel awake. Mom made fun of Rebel because he was so old you expected moths to fly off him when you patted his back.

That's the main thing I remember from those early rides at three or four years old, rocking back and forth and trying to stay in the saddle as I drifted off to sleep. I remember more than one occasion when Daddy lifted me off Rebel's back and into the saddle in front of him so he could hold me for the ride back to the barn, because I was in danger of falling off my own saddle. I had been rocked to sleep every moment of my existence from the time any sort of consciousness bloomed in my mother's womb, since she worked cattle on horseback every day she was pregnant with me, so the lumbering, swaying rhythm of the old horse sent me to la-la-land every time. Mom would have been there on those rides, but she was always bouncing around on some wilder, younger horse. I imagine her bucking around in the ditch, saying shhhhh, shhhh to a frightened two-year-old who'd never seen traffic before. Mom was the one who did the actual training, but Daddy got the credit. He was like her "manager" or something.

I never saw Daddy ride a mare at all. He was too macho for that—as if his massive (not) macho frame was too much for a delicate mare to carry. He preferred to manhandle the studs, the ones Mom rode every day, schooling them for hours, speaking softly to them and teaching them subtle signals with her legs. When it was just us, the regular folk around the barn, Daddy would stand at the fence and yell instructions at Mom while she rode around and around making figures-of-eight on rich men's horses. It makes me dizzy to think of how many figure-eights she made day after day after day in some dusty arena. On days when there was anybody else around, though, Daddy would saddle the finest stallion in the barn for himself. It made no difference to him whether it was a horse he knew at all. No horse had ever been born that he couldn't ride. Then he'd pull the bit too hard and inadvertently jab the horse with a spur, and the rodeo would start. He wasn't even in the saddle when Texon Bull, a particularly crazy young stud horse they'd taken to Texas A&M for a workshop they were leading started his own demonstration of how not to handle a young horse. Daddy never normally rode Texon

Bull, but Mom had four young horses along, and she couldn't ride them all at the same time.

Daddy pulled the reins up tight and stuck his left foot in the stirrup, but the minute his right foot left the ground, before he had a chance to swing it over the saddle, the horse took off sideways, with his eyes rolling showing a white ring all the way around them. Daddy had one leg in the stirrup, and the other leg trailing along while that green-broke stud shied and reared up, nearly taking out the pickup's taillight. It was a miracle neither man nor horse was injured. As usual, Mom was on some high-strung mare skittering across the parking lot in the other direction. I can hear her yelling, "Get out of the horse's mouth, Goddamn it!" Meanwhile, her horse was running away, so her voice was trailing off in the distance.

No, I'd place Daddy in Keen's song somewhere before my time, and maybe before Mom's time. He'd have been crossing a pasture to some lady friend, no doubt, and he was riding the broodmare because he was out of gas, maybe. I think he would have been in Junction, Texas. I don't remember many dandelions out there—more like prickly-pear, mesquite, and cedar trees, with rattlesnakes and scorpions hiding in the shade of the big round rocks that littered the terrain.

Daddy leased a big old ranch on the banks of the Llano River where he ran goats and sheep with the help of a team of illegal immigrants that came and went through the year as they got picked up and sent home only to return a few months later. The same guys came back season on season. They were friends, and Daddy took care that their money got to their families. Mom wrote about them watching out for her when she was alone out there—always from a distance, respectful. They had a bunkhouse away from the main house. There was a joke about how the border patrol would catch them because the trees weren't big enough. They'd run to hide under the same tree when they heard the planes coming because there weren't that many big trees around, but the horses' butts sticking out would give them away.

Anyway, back to Daddy and the broodmare and the stud colt named Willie. If I really think about it, I see that Daddy wouldn't have been out of gas; he would have chosen to ride that broodmare across the canyon to the neighbor's place while the husband was away. That's the sort of thing Daddy would do—sneak a quickie while the husband was away. He might have saddled up the old mare because nobody would miss her or wonder at her being away from the barn because she lived in the pasture with the other mares and their foals. Heck, I can imagine Daddy riding across the canyon bareback with just a rope halter on the old mare. Even less suspicious if anyone should notice the mare and her colt in the neighbor's pasture for an afternoon.

It's the black cloud coming yonder that puts the twist in Keen's tale. This is where Daddy could have gotten caught. You didn't play with rain in the hill country. Flash flooding is still very much a thing out there, and if there was a storm cloud coming, Daddy would have been racing to get to the right side of the canyon ahead of the rain, but, of course, it's hard to race anywhere with a stud colt trailing behind. Daddy was a straight up scoundrel: God's gift to women, at least in his own mind. I tell folks he had a zipper problem, because he rarely met a pretty woman he didn't try to screw, metaphorically or physically. You might say he rode his women hard and put his horses up wet.

So, suppose he got stuck on the wrong side of the canyon. It's a halfway decent cover story. The husband across the canyon comes home and there stands Daddy with a rope halter in his hand, the mare and colt in the man's pasture, but no other means of transportation. The lie would roll right off Daddy's tongue as he explained in good-ol'-boy language to his fellow rancher how the mare and colt had gotten out, the wife had caught them, then driven to get Daddy so he could ride the mare home, just like neighbors do out in the country. It sounded simple. Daddy could fabricate on the fly with the best of them. He must have had a great poker face to cover his nerves while he waited to see if some husband or other was dumb enough to fall for his story.

My grandmother taught me about the devil beating his wife when the sun shone through the raindrops. It was Keen, however, who taught me that the beating took place with a silver chain. I can see the picture in my mind, clear as day... Daddy riding that old broodmare bareback with a rope halter and lead rope looped around her neck. I can see him looking back to call the colt—his voice was lovely. And in an odd way, I can see through Willie's eyes what he looked like, because that's what it looked like when he'd tow me and Rebel along behind him when I was little. He'd turn to look back at us, click his tongue, and say, "Come on," in the sing-songy voice he reserved for animals. Rebel never got in a hurry, just trailed along behind.

Screenplay

Janna Jones

"Feelin' Good Again—Waiting for You"

INT. BLESSED BEAUTY SALON - DAY

A hair stylist COOKIE (40s) who has an angelic, bohemian style is standing at her booth working on a client, JOELLEN (50s).On a shelf at her booth is a framed photo of BOBBY (40s). The photo looks old, but it is clear from the photo that he is a handsome man. Other items at her booth are a hair dryer and some sprays and shampoos and conditioners.

Cookie is cutting Joellen's hair, but there is not any hair on the floor.

Joellen raises her head and looks in the mirror. There is nothing but light where her reflection should be. It doesn't seem to surprise her. While Cookie is working on Joellen's hair, Joellen looks around the salon, which is buzzing, and it is a happy, busy place.

One stylist, SUZI (60's), is drying her client's hair, but the hair dryer doesn't seem to be plugged in. Still, the sound of the dryer is loud. The other stylists MARGO (80s), SAYLOR (20s), and PATTY (60s) are cutting their clients' hair, but there is no hair anywhere on the floor.

CECILIA (60s) one of the stylists, comes out

from the break room and heads straight to Cookie.

Cookie stops cutting Joellen's hair and looks at Cecilia.

                COOKIE
    What is it? You look like you've
    seen a ghost.

The hair salon gets quieter.

                CECILIA
    I've received word. Bobby is on
    his way.

Then the hair salon gets dead quiet. Cookie looks at his photo. And then back at Cecilia.

                COOKIE
    Are you sure? Do you think he's
    OK?

                CECILIA
    Of course, I'm sure. And no, he's
    probably not OK in this moment.
    But he will be, Cookie, you know
    that.

Cookie lays her scissors down. She grabs her phone.

                COOKIE
    Dear God in heaven.

                CECILIA
    Honey, you checking your tracker?

Cookie is looking down at her phone. She nods.

                  COOKIE
    I'm too nervous; I can't focus.

Joellen unclips her cape, hands it to Cecilia and gets up from her chair.

                  JOELLEN
    Now is not the time for you to be worrying about my hair.

Cookie isn't paying attention to Joellen. She lets out a yelp.

                  JOELLEN
    What is it?

                  COOKIE
    He is definitely on his way.

Suzi trots over.

                  SUZI
    When?

                  COOKIE
    It's not clear. What do I do?

                  SUZI
    Why don't you go home? Cecilia and I can cover for you.

Cookie looks down at her phone again.

                    COOKIE
          I wish I had an updated tracker. I
          feel awful for him. Poor baby.

                    CECILIA
          He'll be fine.

Cookie looks down at her phone again.

                    COOKIE
          Looks like it could be tonight.

The other stylists have completely stopped
their work and are staring at Cookie.

                    JOELLEN
          You need to go home and get ready.
          I'll take you home. You're in no
          shape to get there on your own.

Margo, Saylor, and Patty gather around
Cookie.

                    SAYLOR
          What are you going to wear?

Cookie just stares at her phone.

                    MARGO
          Is he going to move in with you?

                    PATTY
          Have you talked to his friends?

                    MARGO
          He's coming tonight?

SAYLOR
              Will the party be tonight?

Cookie crumbles. She starts to cry. Cecilia
hugs Cookie; she pats her on the head.

                    CECILIA
              Too many questions, gals.

                    PATTY
              But what can we do to help?

                    COOKIE
              I don't know!

She starts to cry again.

                    CECILIA
              Poor angel. She's overwhelmed.

INT. COOKIE'S KITCHEN - DAY

Cookie and Joellen are sitting at the kitchen table. The kitchen is mostly pink. The walls are pink, the cupboards are too, and even the kitchen table and chairs are pink.

Cookie and Joellen are drinking tea out of golden teacups.

                    COOKIE
              This place is way too pink.

Joellen grins.

                    JOELLEN
          Honey, I don't think Bobby is going
          to care what color the kitchen is.

Cookie nods.

                    COOKIE
          The bedroom is pink too, you know.

Joellen shakes her head.

                    JOELLEN
          Everybody gets nervous like this.
          Before Ronnie showed up, I thought
          I was going to throw up.

Cookie laughs.

                    JOELLEN
          We had the wildest time when he
          got here. I won't go into the
          details. Except to say, he'd been
          sick before he came, you know, but
          then he wasn't.

She winks at Cookie.

                    COOKIE
          I don't think Bobby's been sick.

                    JOELLEN
          Huh. I wonder.

                    COOKIE
          I always told him that motorcycle
          would be the death of him.

They sit and sip their tea.

>   JOELLEN
> Could be. Honey, I have to take
> off. Ronnie still thinks I am at
> the hair salon.

Cookie nods.

>   COOKIE
> What do I do?

>   JOELLEN
> Well, I'd keep your eye on the
> tracker and figure out what you
> are going to wear. And you should
> probably call your mom. The rest
> can wait until he gets here.

>   COOKIE
> The rest?

>   JOELLEN
> Don't change the color of the
> condo or add a new addition this
> afternoon. You and Bobby can do
> that together.

Cookie laughs and nods. They get up from the table and walk to the front door. They open the front door and all we can see is the brightest of gold lights. They hug and then Joellen disappears into the light.

INT. COOKIE'S BEDROOM - DAY

Cookie is lying on her king size bed. Like the kitchen, most everything in the room is pink. The walls are pink. The headboard is pink. There is a tall pink mirror leaning against the wall. It would seem like Cookie's reflection would be in the mirror, but all it reflects is a golden light.

She is staring at her tracker. There is a constant beeping signal. The icon, which is a pair of wings, seems to be slowly moving toward a destination. Looking more closely, the destination reads "here." She gets off the bed and walks over to her closet and opens the door.

What hangs in the closet is a bit of a surprise. There are 40, maybe 50 dresses, that all look like the one she has on. She looks at a few of them, scrutinizing them. Then she pulls one of them out of the closet. She holds it to her body and then begins to dance around the room with it. As soon as she begins to dance, a song begins to play.

> SONG
> Packed my suitcase and I racked my brain Bought a ticket on a late night train Took a taxi through the pouring rain I'm coming home to you Flew from Boston out to San Jose/ Saw our old friends in Monterey Bay/ When they asked me if I'd like to stay I said I'm

                    SONG (cont.)
          coming home to you/ I'm coming
          home Made up my mind that's what
          I'm gonna do Can't love nobody on
          the telephone I'm coming home to
          you.

Cookie waltzes around the room with her
dress. As she passes by the mirror, we cannot
see her reflection, but we can see a golden
light, which intensifies as Cookie gets closer to the mirror, and then the light pulsates
with the beat of the music.

INT. COOKIE'S BATHROOM

Cookie is in her pink bathtub. She is covered
in bubbles. Her eyes are closed. When she
opens them, she picks up her phone. She looks
at the tracker. The beeping has stopped. The
icon is no longer moving toward "here." The
signal is back at "there." Cookie starts to
wail. She, along with her phone, submerges
under the water in the bathtub.

INT. COOKIE'S KITCHEN - DAY

Cookie is sitting at her kitchen table. Her
hair is wrapped in a pink towel. She has a
pink robe on. She picks up her phone off the
table and looks at the screen and without
effort BUTTON (70s) appears.
She looks to be outside, as she has a hat on,
and mighty winds are blowing her hair around.

                    COOKIE
          Mom.

                    BUTTON
          Hi darling!

Cookie starts to cry.

                    BUTTON
          What is it, sweetheart?

                    COOKIE
          Bobby was on his way here.

                    BUTTON
          Fabulous!

                    COOKIE
          But the icon stopped moving and
          now he's back there.

Cookie cries some more.

                    BUTTON
          Oh Cookie. I'm so sorry. That does
          happen sometimes.

Cookie sobs.

                    COOKIE
          Can you come home?

Button cocks her head. She looks at Cookie
with compassion.

BUTTON
Honey, I can't. I'm helping some-
body at the top of Mt. Everest.

COOKIE
Where's Dad?

BUTTON
Deep in the Amazon.

Cookie nods.

BUTTON
You know how he is. But we will
get home as soon as we can.

COOKIE
OK.

BUTTON
Sweetie, we love you, and we
always have and always will.

Cookie sobs.

COOKIE
I love you too.

BUTTON
Look at the wonderful life you've
created for yourself here.

COOKIE
I know but—

                    BUTTON
          You are actually fine by yourself,
          right?

                    COOKIE
          I guess but—

                    BUTTON
          Enjoy this time. Believe me when
          he gets here, you're not going to
          have a moment to yourself.

Cookie laughs a little.

                    BUTTON
          So be patient. He'll get here when
          he gets here.

Button waves goodbye.

                    BUTTON
          I've got to go sweetheart. This
          hiker is in big trouble.

She disappears from the screen.

Cookie's phone dings.

A new face appears on the screen before Cookie can even put her phone down.

It's GEORGE (30s). He's handsome, with long hair and a goatee.

                    GEORGE
          Hey you.

                    COOKIE
          He's not coming.

                    GEORGE
          I know. But we're going to have a
          party anyway.

Cookie looks at him with disbelief.

                    COOKIE
          Don't even ask me to come—

George laughs.

                    GEORGE
          Listen, I want Bobby to get here
          too. But it's not working out that
          way today.

Cookie sighs.

                    GEORGE
          Did you talk to Mom?

Cookie rolls her eyes.

                    COOKIE
          Yes.

They both snort.

                    GEORGE
          Our parents are the

GEORGE (cont.)
weirdest. They take their jobs so seriously.

Finally, Cookie smiles.

GEORGE
Seriously, Cooks, just come out tonight. We will celebrate Bobby's almost-arrival.

COOKIE
I don't know.

GEORGE
Come on. I want to give my little sister a big hug.

COOKIE
I miss him so much.

GEORGE
We all do.

COOKIE
I keep checking the stupid tracker.

GEORGE
Come out tonight and leave your phone at home. The Boys from Silver City are playing.

COOKIE
I'll think about it.

                         GEORGE
          Just do it. I'll see you in a lit-
          tle while.

George disappears from the screen.

Cookie puts her phone down and puts her head in her hands.

INT. COOKIE'S KITCHEN—EVENING

Cookie is dressed to go out. She looks gorgeous though not particularly happy.

She has her phone in her hand. She is looking at the tracker.

The tracker is not beeping and the icon is not moving.

Cookie sighs. She puts her hand on the door knob. She opens the door a tiny bit. Light pours in. She takes her hand off the door knob and turns around. She puts her phone on the kitchen table.

                         COOKIE
          I'll be back.

She turns around and walks through the door.

She shuts the door behind her and the light disappears again.

The tracker on the kitchen table beeps.

The icon on the tracker starts to move, rather quickly, toward "here."

INT. MR. BLUES - NIGHT

Cookie and George are on some stairs listening to the BOYS OF SILVER CITY which include a GUITARIST/SINGER (70s), BASS GUITARIST/SINGER (40s) and a KEYBOARDIST/SINGER (60s).

PERKINS (80s) is sitting on a stool, watching BUTCH (60s) and JIMMY JOHN (50s) playing pool.

Cecilia, Suzi, and Margo are standing near the table watching the boys play.

They look up at the stairs and smile at Cookie and George and wave.

Saylor walks up to her parents DAN (60s) and MARGARITA (60s) who are dancing.

The three of them start dancing together.

Joellen and RONNIE (60s) walk in. Joellen spots Cookie and George and waves at them.

Saylor stops dancing with her parents and climbs up the stairs to Cookie and George.

                    SAYLOR
    Wanna dance?

George looks at Cookie. Cookie smiles.

                          COOKIE
          Go ahead.

George hugs his sister and takes Saylor's hand, and they walk down the stairs together.

Saylor and George begin to dance. It looks like they've been dancing partners for eternity.

Cookie watches the scene and smiles.

Everybody on the floor is dancing--Joellen and Ronnie, Saylor and George, Perkins and Margo, Butch and Cecilia, Jimmy John and Suzi, and Dan and Margarita.

Everybody is dancing but Cookie. She just listens to the Boys of the Silver City sing her favorite song. She sways to the music with her eyes closed.

                  BOYS OF SILVER CITY
Packed my suitcase and I racked my brain
Bought a ticket on a late night train
Took a taxi through the pouring rain
I'm coming home to you
Flew from Boston out to San Jose
Saw our old friends in Monterey Bay
When they asked me if I'd like to stay
I said I'm coming home to you
I'm coming home
Made up my mind that's what I'm gonna do
Can't love nobody on the telephone
I'm coming home to you.
When she opens her eyes, the dancing has stopped.

The boys are playing pool again. Perkins is back on his stool.

Cookie is about to walk down the stairs when she notices the door open. An abundance of light temporarily blinds her, but after the door closes again, she sees somebody walk in.

Because of the light, she doesn't recognize him for a half of a second. Though he looks around the room like he already knows everybody.

She gasps.

It's Bobby.

He puts his head down for a second as he puts his hand in his pocket and pulls out a wad of cash.

He looks surprised to find the money. He stuffs it back in his pocket, and as he does, he raises his head and smiles.

He surveys the room.

He sees Cookie.

His jaw drops.

She breaks into a grin.

The Boys of Silver City stop singing.

Everyone stops talking or playing pool or

whatever they were doing. Everything and everyone is frozen except for Cookie and Bobby.

Cookie walks down the stairs.

Bobby walks across the room.

Bobby picks up Cookie and spins her around.

>BOBBY
>Have I told you lately how much I love you?

Cookie giggles.

>COOKIE
>It's been a minute.

And then The Boys of Silver City start playing and singing again.

Everyone unfreezes.

Bobby stops spinning Cookie and takes her in his arms and starts to dance.

Everyone returns to the dance floor.

>BOYS OF SILVER CITY
>*When they asked me if I'd like to stay*
>*I said I'm coming home to you*
>*I'm coming home*
>*Made up my mind that's what I'm gonna do*
>*Can't love nobody on the telephone*
>*I'm coming home to you*

                    BOBBY
          Babe, I don't know exactly what's
          going on, but this feels like
          heaven.

Cookie laughs.

                    COOKIE
          That's exactly what is going on.

                    BOBBY
          Me and you, we're in heaven?

                    COOKIE
          Yep.

                    BOBBY
          Holy cow, Cooks.

Everyone is dancing.

The Boys of Silver City continue to play and sing--like they think they are the Tabernacle choir.

Contributors

Alan Birkelbach is a Texas native, raised on the food holy trinity of Barbecue, Tex-Mex, and kolaches. Appointed the Texas Poet Laureate in 2005, he is author of twelve books of poetry, including the latest, *The National Parks: A Century of Grace* with fellow Texas Poet Laureate karla k. morton. He currently lives in New Mexico but misses good Texas music and Whataburger.

Heath Bowen's poems and stories have appeared in literary journals *I-70 review*, *Dead Mule School of Southern Literature*, *River Poets Journal*, *Muddy River Poetry Review*, *miniskirt magazine*, and *Eckerd Review*. When not writing prose or poetry, Heath teaches Literature & Labor History at a community college in the Midwest.

Rick Campbell is a poet and essayist living on Alligator Point, Florida. His most recent book of poetry is *Fish Streets Before Dawn* (Press 53). A collection of essays, *Sometimes the Light* (Main Street Rag Press) was published in 2022. Other poetry collections include *Provenance*; *Gunshot, Peacock, Dog*; *The History of Steel*; *Dixmont*; *Setting the World in Order*; *The Traveler's Companion*, and *A Day's Work*. His poems and essays have appeared in many journals and anthologies, including *Georgia Review*, *Fourth River*, *Kestrel*, *Alabama Literary Review*, and *Prairie Schooner*. He's won a Pushcart Prize and an NEA Fellowship in Poetry. He teaches in the University of Nevada-Reno's MFA program.

Greg Clary is a retired college professor born and raised in Turkey Creek, West Virginia. He now resides in the northwestern Pennsylvania wilds where he enjoys cathead biscuits, an occasional two fingers of Jameson over one cube of ice, and people who can ease into conversation without taking it over. His photographs and poetry have appeared in many publications including *The Sun Magazine*, *Looking at Appalachia*, *Rattle*, *The Watershed Journal*, *Pine Mountain Sand & Gravel*, *Rye Whiskey Review*, *Waccamaw Journal*, *Trailer Park Quarterly*, *Northern Appalachian Review*, *Change Seven*, *Appalachian Lit*, and *Hole in the Head Review*.

Andrew E. Coats has been a professional singer/songwriter/guitarist for over 30 years. His six albums as an independent musician (as "Andy Coats") are mainly of original songs mixed with his interpretations of roots and blues songs, available on major streaming platforms and www.andycoats.com. He graduated summa cum laude from the UNC (Chapel Hill) with a BA in philosophy then earned MA and PhD degrees in philosophy from the

University of California, Riverside. Currently, he pursues the field of Artificial Intelligence/Machine Learning, and is currently writing an essay for an anthology entitled *Interrogating AI*.

Michael Amos Cody was born in the South Carolina Lowcountry and raised in the North Carolina highlands. He spent his twenties writing songs in Nashville and his thirties getting an education. He is the author of the novel *Gabriel's Songbook* (Pisgah Press, 2017) and the story collection *A Twilight Reel* (Pisgah Press, 2021), which won the Short Story/Anthology category of the Feathered Quill Book Awards in 2022. His novel *Streets of Nashville* is scheduled to be published in early 2025 by Madville Publishing. He lives in Jonesborough, TN, with wife Leesa where he teaches literature at East Tennessee State University.

Ron Cooper is a native of the Low Country South Carolina swamps that are so thick airplanes must shift into low gear when flying over. He moved to Florida in 1988, and is the author of five books as well as poems, short stories, and critical essays in many journals. He holds a BA from the College of Charleston, an MA from the University of South Carolina, and a PhD from Rutgers. His novel *Purple Jesus* was called by the *Washington Post* "a literary event of the first magnitude." His fourth novel, *All My Sins Remembered*, won a Florida Book Award. He lives in Ocala, FL, with his wife Sandra and their kids.

Sandra Johnson Cooper, Senior Professor of Literature and Composition at the College of Central Florida, is a published poet, a long-time writing teacher, and a past member of the Board of Directors of the Florida Literary Arts Coalition. She is originally from Horse Creek Valley, South Carolina, home to the world's largest pond. She lives with her husband, Ron, their children, and an assortment of animals in Ocala, FL.

Kimberly Parish Davis is the director and founder of Madville Publishing. She sometimes teaches English Composition, Creative Writing, and Technical writing, and spent five years on the editorial staff of Texas Review Press. Her fiction, creative nonfiction, and poetry have been published in various literary journals. Her short story collection, *Trust Issues*, is forthcoming from Cornerstone Press. Find her online at kpdavis.com.

Donna Wojnar Dzuurilla, MFA, graduated from Carlow University where she studied at Trinity College in Dublin, Ireland. Her work has appeared in the *Anthology of Appalachian Writers Ann Pancake Volume 16*, *Backbone Mountain Review*, *Northern Appalachia Review*, *Voices from the Attic* anthology series, *Rune*, the *Pittsburgh Post-Gazette*, *Presence*, and other publications. Upcoming publications include work in the *Shelia-Na-Gig Fiction Anthology Volume II* (Shelia-Na-Gig, 2024), and poetry in *The Gulf Tower Forecasts Rain Anthology* (City of Asylum, 2025). Her photography will be featured in the upcoming volume of *Trailer Park Quarterly*, an online poetry journal.

Rupert Fike's second collection of poems, *Hello the House* (Snake Nation Press) was named one of the "Books All Georgians Should Read, 2018" by The Georgia Center for the Book. He was a finalist as Georgia Author of the Year after his first collection, *Lotus Buffet* (Brick Road Poetry Press, 2011). His stories and poems have appeared in *The Southern Poetry Review*, *The Sun*, *storySouth*, *Kestrel*, *Scalawag Magazine*, *Georgetown Review*, *A&U America's AIDS Magazine*, *Flannery O'Connor Review*, *Duende*, *Buddhist Poetry Review*, and others.

Patrick Michael Finn is the author of *A Martyr for Suzy Kosasovich*, *From the Darkness Right Under Our Feet*, and *A Place for Snakes to Breed*. His fiction has appeared in *Ploughshares*, *TriQuarterly*, *Quarterly West*, and *The Best American Mystery Stories*. He has also received distinguished story citations in the *Pushcart Prize* anthology and *The Best American Short Stories*. Finn is currently at work on a new novel, *And Lead Me Not*, and a collection of short stories tentatively titled *Shoot You Every Second of Your Life*. He lives in Mesa, Arizona, with his wife, poet Valerie Bandura, and their son.

Cal Freeman is the music editor of *The Museum of Americana: A Literary Review* and author of the books *Fight Songs* (Eyewear 2017) and *Poolside at the Dearborn Inn* (R&R Press 2022). His writing has appeared or is forthcoming in journals including *Image*, *The Poetry Review*, *Verse Daily*, *North American Review*, *Oxford American*, and *Hippocampus*. He is a recipient of the Devine Poetry Fellowship, winner of Passages North's Neutrino Prize, and a finalist for the River Styx International Poetry Prize. Born and raised in Detroit, he teaches at Oakland University and serves as Writer-In-Residence with InsideOut Literary Arts Detroit.

Scott Gould is the author of five books, including *The Hammerhead Chronicles*, winner of the Eric Hoffer Award for Fiction, and *Things That Crash, Things That Fly*, which won a 2022 Memoir Prize for Books. His latest book is a collection of stories, *Idiot Men*. His work has appeared in a number of publications, including *Kenyon Review*, *Black Warrior Review*, *BULL*, *Pangyrus*, *New Ohio Review*, *Crazyhorse*, *Pithead Chapel*, *Garden & Gun*, and *New Stories from the South*. He lives in Sans Souci, South Carolina, and teaches at the South Carolina Governor's School for the Arts & Humanities.

Bobby Horecka is a lifelong journalist who currently serves as managing editor of five weekly newspapers and contributor to roughly a dozen others. His journalistic works have appeared on every continent over the past 37 years, earning him many awards for writing, photography, and page design. His story collection *Long Gone & Lost* (Madville in 2020) was shortlisted for the Texas Institute of Letters' best first book of fiction award in 2021. Bobby and his wife, Jennifer, live on the south Texas farm where he grew up.

Janna Jones is a professor in the school of Communication at Northern Arizona University. She teaches screenwriting, media criticism, and communication graduate courses. She is the author of the books *The Southern Movie Palace: Rise, Fall, and Resurrection*; *The Past is a Moving Picture: Preserving the Twentieth Century on Film*; and *The Spirit of the City: Marshall Fredericks Sculptures in Detroit*. She has also published essays about film, architecture, design, and preservation and has won more than 100 screenplay awards. When she is not writing or teaching, you can find her at the barn with her horses and mule.

After twenty-four years in Fort Lauderdale, **Carol Parris Krauss** relocated to Virginia to be closer to her family and was honored as a UVA Best New Poet. In 2021, her book *Just a Spit Down the Road* was published by Kelsay. Some venues in which she has publications are *Louisiana Lit*, *One Art*, *Schuylkill Valley Journal*, *storySouth*, and *Highland Park Poetry*, and she was selected for Ghost City Press's 2023 Micro-Chap Summer Series. Her chapbook, *The Old Folks Call it God's Country*, was released by The Poetry Box (2024).

Patti Meredith grew up in Galax, Virginia. Most of her stories are set in the Blue Ridge Mountains, but her debut novel, *South of Heaven*, takes place in the North Carolina Sandhills. She holds an MFA in Creative Writing from the University of Memphis. Her stories have appeared in *Salvation South*, *Appalachian Review*, *Still: The Journal*, and *Mulberry Fork Review*. Patti, her husband Lee, and their springer spaniel, Maggie, are now settled in Chapel Hill.

karla k. morton, is a National Heritage Wrangler Award winner, Spur Award winner, and Foreword Indies National Book Award winner. She is widely published, has sixteen books, and is the 2010 Texas State Poet Laureate and Nominee for the National Cowgirl Hall of Fame.

The honorary Poet in Residence at Abraham Baldwin Agricultural College in Tifton, Georgia, **Jeff Newberry** is an essayist, novelist, and poet. His Pushcart-nominated writing has appeared in a wide variety of journals and magazines, including *South Carolina Review*, *North American Review*, and *Brevity: Concise Nonfiction*. The author of a novel, a chapbook, and two previous collections of poetry, he recently published *How to Talk about the Dead* (Redhawk Publications), a finalist for the Arthur Smith Poetry Prize. He is the vice president of the Southeastern Writers Association.

Garrison M. Somers is a native of New Jersey and a graduate of the College of Charleston, South Carolina. He is editor of *The Blotter Magazine* (Durham, NC), online 'zines *Four Quarters* and *Corner Bar*, and author of the novel *Livie's Lilies* and a memoir of collected essays, *Upwards, Dad Words*. He lives with his wife and daughters in Chapel Hill, North Carolina. If you see him on the front porch there, don't be afraid to go up and ask for a cup of coffee.